"A novel in the form of an ambush—a wildy funny story
that becomes mysteriously touching and ponderable before
the end. . . . I urge you not to miss it."
—BENJAMIN DEMOTT, *The Atlantic Monthly*

"Ms. Reich's book lives. Her characters love, marry,
give birth, get stoned, commit bigamy. In the end,
[her] comic vision gives the last word to life . . .
A rapturous celebration."
—HUGH NISSENSON, *The New York Times Book Review*

"Tova Reich's *Master of the Return* is a novel in
the form of an ambush—a wildly funny story that becomes
mysteriously touching and ponderable before the end . . . Tova
Reich is a marvelously enigmatic original, and there are effects in
her book that are beyond casual summoning,
secrets reason can't reach."
—*The Atlantic*

PRAISE FOR *MY HOLOCAUST*

"Serious and hilarious and utterly scathing . . .
Tova Reich is the master of fury's return."
—*Washington Post Book World*

"*My Holocaust* is a ferocious work of serious satiric genius.
I believe it to be one of the most penetrating social and political
novels of the early twenty-first century, next to which the
last century's *Animal Farm* is a mere bleat."
—CYNTHIA OZICK

THE HOUSE OF LOVE AND PRAYER

and other stories

TOVA REICH

SEVEN STORIES PRESS
NEW YORK · OAKLAND

"The Lost Girl" was published in *Harper's* in August 1995, for which it won The National Magazine Award for Fiction. It was included in *The Norton Anthology of Jewish American Literature*, edited by Jules Chametzky, John Felstiner, Hilene Flanzbaum, and Kathryn Hellerstein (W. W. Norton and Co., 2001).

The following stories first appeared in *Conjunctions*: "Forbidden City" (Fall 2004), "The Plot" (Spring 2007), and "The Page Turner" (March 2019).

"The Third Generation" first appeared as a short story in *The Atlantic* (March 2000) and was later included in the anthology *Faith*, edited by C. Michael Curtis (Harper Collins, 2003). In altered form and renamed "The Holocaust Princess," it became the first chapter of my 2007 novel *My Holocaust*.

"Dedicated to the Dead" appeared in *AGNI* (October 15, 2005) and was later included in the anthology *The New Diaspora: The Changing Landscape of American Jewish Fiction*, edited by Victoria Aarons, Avinoam J. Patt, and Mark Schechner (Wayne State University Press, 2015).

"Dead Zone" was published by *Ploughshares* as a "Ploughshares Solo" (June 17, 2015).

SEVEN STORIES PRESS www.sevenstories.com

Library of Congress Cataloging-in-Publication Data

Names: Reich, Tova, author.
Title: The house of love and prayer : and other stories / Tova Reich.
Description: Regular edition (rg). | New York ; Oakland : Seven Stories
    Press, [2023]
Identifiers: LCCN 2022053231 | ISBN 9781644212745 (hardcover) | ISBN
    9781644212752 (electronic)
Classification: LCC PS3568.E4763 H68 2023 | DDC 813/.54--dc23
LC record available at https://lccn.loc.gov/2022053231

College professors and high school and middle school teachers may order free examination copies of Seven Stories Press titles. Visit https://www.sevenstories.com/pg/resources-academics or email academics@sevenstories.com.

Printed in the USA.

9 8 7 6 5 4 3 2 1

To Avrumie

CONTENTS

The Lost Girl

It was not the first time that Rabbi Yehiel Berman had had dealings with the media, but on all those previous occasions it had been with what he classified as the "Anglo-Jewish press," and to them he could comment in a kind of shorthand. By them he could count on being understood. Whatever was spoken, was spoken within the walls of the family compound, as it were. He would be given the benefit of the doubt, and, ultimately, if necessary, he would be forgiven. But in the matter of the lost girl, Feigie Singer, and all the publicity attendant on that mess, it was no less than the mighty *New York Times* that had approached him, and Rabbi Berman had made the grievous error of taking seriously an unquestioned conviction lodged many years earlier in his consciousness and accepted by him in innocent good faith—namely, the fact that the *Times* was a Jewish organ.

So when the *Times* reporter approached him for a comment on the Singer case, he had spoken openly, as one speaks to a brother, or at the very least a cousin. Because even a cousin several times removed would understand that there are two forms of speech—one meant for the inner precincts and the other for the outside sphere. And even that cousin, however many times cut off, would recognize that it is in their mutual interest to take the words spoken within the chambers and refine them for consumption by a hostile world where the one thing you could depend on was any excuse to pounce on the Jews—"All Jews irregardless," as Rabbi Berman liked to put it—no matter how distant the cousinship. The least Rabbi Berman could have expected from that reporter, a Jewish fellow named Sean Markowitz, as a matter of fact, was to apply some basic common sense in the interest of Jewish survival. As Rabbi Berman admonished this traitor afterward, when it was already too late, when his so-called offensive remark had been spread far and wide in the newspaper without commentary or spin, in a bitter phone call at that time the rabbi had counseled Markowitz that he would do well in the future to recite the Shema with intense fervor, to pray "Hear, O Israel" each and every time he sat down at his desk to write even a single word about the Jewish people, in order to remind himself of his awesome responsibility, his heavy burden, lest he do, as he had certainly done with the rabbi's quote, severe harm to his own tribe and, by extension, whether he acknowledged this or not, to himself.

Above all, the rabbi had sought to drum a little empathy into the uselessly educated brain of this arrogant kid. Do not judge your friend until you reach his place, the sages teach. And who, who in this world, could ever imagine what it must be like to be in Rabbi Berman's position? To be the principal of an all-girls high school, to bear the weight of molding and shaping, day in and day out, the minds and souls of three hundred girls in the most difficult ages of fourteen through eighteen, to be charged with preparing these specimens for the critical task of Jewish wifehood and motherhood, in short, for the continuation of our people—this was the hard reality that Rabbi Berman had to face, a reality quite beyond the comprehension of the Markowitzes of this world. Did Markowitz realize, for instance, that by the age of twenty, God willing, most or all of these girls would already be married off to yeshiva boys who sit and learn all day? Some were even engaged in their junior year of high school. A year at a women's seminary in Israel after graduation, night classes at Brooklyn College, some secretarial work or maybe something in computers, marking time, as it were, and then, with God's help, they would be settled away. By twenty, many were already pushing a baby in a carriage down Thirteenth Avenue with another on the way, and if they were not fixed up by then it would truly be *okh und vey*, a serious problem, bad news for these girls and their families, a looming calamity in fact, because already a new crop of eighteen-year-olds would be coming up, and the chances these old goods had then of fulfilling the destiny that he, Rabbi Berman, and the institution he headed were preparing them for would be drastically reduced, reduced exponentially.

Now, was this a reality that Markowitz and his ilk could absorb? Did Markowitz have even an inkling of an idea of what it meant to be in the rabbi's shoes? Statistically speaking, in any given week at the school, the rabbi had once calculated, approximately one quarter of these girls, about seventy-five girls in all, had their periods. Could anyone imagine what it must be like to be living in the middle of all that? Sometimes he felt as if he were drowning in a thick soup. The constant smell of talcum, of old perspiration in woolen sweaters, the endless dieting and self-dissatisfaction, the pimples, the greasy hair, the preening, the sudden bursts of weeping, the shrieking, the jumping up and down, the hugging and kissing, the gossip, envy, rivalry, intrigue, the cliques, the moodiness, the obligation to chide this or that one for wearing makeup, shoes that made noise, colors that were too bright, sleeves that were too short, for snatching the excuse of warm weather not to wear any stockings at all—an obligation that naturally carried with it the necessity of looking closely at these growing girls, when for the sake of the purity of his spirit he would, of course, have preferred not to—all of this was a headache beyond description.

And, to make matters worse, if you didn't count the public high school teachers who came into the building in the late afternoon for the secular subjects, since all the religious classes were taught by married women in wigs and head scarves and hats, he, Rabbi Yehiel Berman, was the only man on the premises the entire day, not including Reb Avraham Washington, the janitor. But Reb Washington was a special case, a black man who had been their custodian for years, who had been so influenced and impressed by the Jewish lifestyle that he had actually converted, married the longtime secretary, the widow Mrs. Halpern, and now he could be seen in his full beard and side curls, shuffling around the facility with his mops and pails, wearing a black felt hat over his black velvet yarmulke and a great fringed ritual garment on top of his white shirt. Yet, in a very real sense, Reb Avraham Washington, no matter how sincere his convictions, could never really be considered a player, and, for all intents and purposes, he, Rabbi Yehiel Berman, was the only male on the scene.

So when the Singer girl had gotten lost that spring during the Lag B'Omer outing, when she had not come out of the woods after wandering for over an hour with all the other girls, when she had not returned to the buses waiting in the parking lot, when, to the rabbi's utter astonishment, the disappearance of this skinny little girl had inspired the extraordinary spectacle of swarms of Hasidim in black garb from Massachusetts to Maryland, as well as other—secular—men, descending on these woods in upstate New York in search of this female, and the whole business had become big news, this guy Markowitz from the *Times* naturally sought out Rabbi Berman, as the principal of the school, for a comment. Markowitz's attitude had been openly hostile and confrontational from the outset. Wasn't the rabbi aware that this particular forest was notoriously confusing, complex, overgrown, filled with traps and illusions? How could he have allowed such young and vulnerable girls to wander in there alone? What form of supervision had been provided for these students, city girls that they were, innocent entirely of raw nature?

And even though Rabbi Berman knew that a wise man answers the first question first and the second second, everything in order, he hastened, in this instance, to take on at once the final query for which he had a ready response. There were fifteen chaperones in charge of the girls, he told Markowitz proudly, trained teachers from our school, one adult per every group of twenty adolescents. He did not add that the women had most likely remained in the parking lot, chatting in clumps—chatting, as usual, about this and that, about children, about where to get the best prices, comparing outfits—while the girls went off into the woods. He assumed that this had been the case, based on his past experience observing teachers in the yard overseeing students during free time, but why should he have volunteered such compromising information to Markowitz if he had not witnessed it with his own eyes? Because, naturally, he himself had not gone on the trip with the student body due to the delicate and essentially forbidden circumstance into which he would have been forced—of riding in close quarters for such a long period of time in the exclusive company of the opposite sex. True, the bus drivers were male, but they, of course, were gentiles.

Then, having successfully cleared away the issue of adequate supervision, Rabbi Berman diplomatically attempted to draw Markowitz closer, to establish some sort of bond of kinship between them, to bring him over to their side. "What kind of name is Sean for a Jewish boy?" he inquired with amused familiarity. Most likely, the rabbi went on to conjecture, he had been named for some ancestor called Samuel, Shmuel—Shmiel or Shmulik, in the Yiddish way. "So tell me, Shmulik," the rabbi said, "when was the last time you put on t'fillin since your bar mitzvah?"

But Markowitz wasn't buying. He persisted in questioning the rabbi, not only about the supervision for the trip—obviously he had found the answer unsatisfactory—but also about all the other arrangements and preparations, and about the steps they had taken upon discovering that a girl was missing, until, in exasperation, and, really, in an attempt, misguided perhaps but well intentioned nonetheless, to bring some relief, some lightness, to a grim situation, Rabbi Berman had come out with the statement that had gotten him into so much trouble. "Look, Shmiel," he said, "we went into the woods with three hundred girls and came out with two hundred ninety-nine. Now, you learned arithmetic. If you consider all girls equal, so that each one is worth the same amount of points, on a final exam that would give you a score of about ninety-nine point seven out of one hundred—a sure A, maybe even an A plus. Not a bad showing in anybody's book—am I right?" For this comment even members of his own community had chastised him, accusing him of insensitivity, of failing to place the proper value on one human life. Rabbi Yehiel Berman had been completely misunderstood.

And, after all, who was this girl Feigie Singer to inspire such a fuss? Of course, she was a human being—that goes without saying. Naturally, she was not a nothing, God forbid. But such a small, timid creature, the youngest in a family of thirteen— her father drove a fruit and vegetable truck, selling door to door, housewives bought from him out of pity. This was a girl who scarcely made any impression at all. You barely noticed her, she was hardly there even when she wasn't lost. It was a wonder, in a way, that they even realized she was missing. In this assessment, which, thank God, the rabbi had had the good sense to refrain from verbalizing, he was nevertheless backed up by two student leaders, Pessie Glick and Dvorah Birnbaum, who told Markowitz that Feigie was an exceptionally quiet girl, afraid of every little thing, you could practically see her heart pounding and fluttering like a naked newborn chick under her blouse, definitely not the type to go wandering off alone in the woods. Oh, they were very worried that something terrible had happened to her, Pessie and Dvorah said.

She had, in fact, been walking with them when she disappeared, cowering and trembling at every little movement and noise. Then, suddenly, they had turned around and Feigie was gone. The woods were extremely tangled and dark and moist. There was a man in there, they reported. They had seen him with their own eyes. Several times they saw him, though not while they were with Feigie. Later, only after she had vanished. He was wearing a uniform of some sort—a forest ranger, they thought—rubber boots, a wide-brimmed hat with a leather band, a heavy wooden stick in his hand. They themselves circled aimlessly for another hour at least after Feigie disappeared, utterly lost and confused, clutching each other's hand, before they had finally, thank God, seen a clearing of light and found their way out into the parking lot.

And these two girls, Rabbi Berman noted, Pessie and Dvorah, were from the school's elite, from very good backgrounds, handsome, well-dressed girls. They would no doubt be married off within a year to excellent prospects from comfortable, well-connected families, families that would support them over the first few years while the boy sat and learned Torah all day and maybe studied at night for an accounting or an actuarial degree and the couple started a family of its own. Little Feigie Singer must have been honored, thrilled, to be allowed to walk in the woods in their company, alongside such important girls, Rabbi Berman was sure. Such, he knew, was the politics of a girls' high school. If it had been the Glick or the Birnbaum girl who had disappeared, it would have been a different story entirely. Whether Markowitz realized it or not, he was getting his inside information from the most prestigious teenage source possible, the cream of the cream. What

Pessie and Dvorah said to him should have put the status of the Singer girl clearly into perspective.

So when the searchers brought Feigie Singer out of the woods nearly three days later, a little hungry, a little tired, a little soiled, but, to the uncritical eye, at least externally undamaged, it was a shock, almost like a blow, to Pessie and Dvorah, and to their entire school community for that matter, and it was a surprise even to the rabbi himself, he had to admit, that she was escorted out like a heroine, like a princess from an ancient tale. Yet even so, even though this meek girl had been welcomed like a celebrity when she was rescued, and masses gathered to dance and rejoice at her salvation, and even though Rabbi Yehiel Berman observed over the ensuing months that she had begun to grow considerably and to ripen, you should excuse me, in a recognizably womanly fashion, he had nevertheless regarded it as necessary at the time of her deliverance to urge her parents to collect notarized letters and affidavits from doctors and other examining authorities testifying to the fact that nothing compromising had happened to her during those days when she had been alone in the woods. This would be a wise precaution, Rabbi Berman had advised, in anticipation of the time, only a few years from now, when they would be seeking a suitable match for her, and the boys' families would recall the event and, naturally, they would pause and they would wonder.

When they found her in the early morning hours of the third day, she was inside the hollow shell of the dead tree trunk in which she had finally settled to await her fate. It was like a cradle, she imagined, high and protected on each side, soft and damp in the interior with decaying matter that peeled off and clung to her clothing and tangled in her hair, and when she curled up to sleep it seemed to her to be almost rocking. Her parents, of course, would have realized that she had not come home, but what resources could they muster to try to find her, downtrodden and careworn as they were? They were not the kind of people who liked to call attention to themselves, and a daughter who does not return home, that was in a way a shameful thing, not something they would want to get around. Pessie and Dvorah would probably have noticed that she was gone, most likely they would have reported her missing, though while she was walking beside them in the woods, they seemed hardly to have noticed her. They didn't even bother to shake her off or to lower their voices to whisper their secrets but went on chatting intimately with each other as if they were entirely alone.

They really were magnificent girls, Pessie and Dvorah, tall and stately, Pessie with her red hair streaming down her back, held with a black velvet barrette, Dvorah's rich, dark curls framing the smooth paleness of her face. These were girls truly at the cusp of their bridal season, beautifully packaged, as it were, in designer clothing that their mothers single-mindedly hunted out for them from fashionable, bejeweled women in gorgeous blond pageboy wigs who operated discount boutiques in the basements of their Borough Park homes. For her part, Feigie was wearing the long, drab khaki-colored skirt and the well-washed blouse with the tiny yellow flowers and sleeves buttoned at the wrists handed down from her sisters, white kneesocks, and sneakers. Her only ornaments were the small gold studs in her ears, which her mother had insisted she have pierced, and the gold ring with the tiny amethyst birthstone that she had been given three months earlier, on her fourteenth birthday. Pessie had milky pearls in her ears, and Dvorah elegant gold hoops, and they were each carrying fine leather pocketbooks slung stylishly over their shoulders, while she, Feigie, had all of her possessions for this outing—her cream cheese and jelly sandwich wrapped in aluminum foil, her old Instamatic camera, her little prayer book, and a few dollars—in a lump at the bottom of the plastic Waldbaum's shopping bag that she clutched in her hand.

She could never imagine ever flowering as gloriously as they, even in three years' time, even when she, too, would become a senior. She could never imagine ever being able to converse as amusingly or as easily or as confidently. How did they always know the right thing to say? She walked along silently beside them, trying to absorb every detail of their manner and speech, trying not to embarrass herself by starting at every sound and rustle in the woods, straining to keep up even though she was growing increasingly weary and alarmed as they penetrated deeper and deeper among the trees, her heart beating so that she was afraid they could hear it, a dragging ache radiating down her back, across her belly, into her thighs.

Would she ever possess the power to talk as fluidly, as brazenly, about Rabbi Berman for example, as they did? It seemed to Feigie to be a veritable gift, quite beyond her. They actually called him Berman. Last week Berman had asked her if she was wearing stockings, Dvorah told Pessie. Would you believe? He even put out his hand as if to slide it down her leg. Just checking, you know. Dvorah giggled. Hadn't he ever heard of sheer pantyhose, for heaven's sake? Yeah, Pessie said, just two days ago Berman stopped her in the hallway and told her that her earrings were too long and dangly. He looked like he was about to rip them right out of her ears. There was definitely something wrong with the guy.

What could Feigie possibly contribute to the conversation? Rabbi Berman never looked at her, and ever since their one and only conversation, when it had been her turn to be called into his office in the early autumn for the routine interview with each new freshman, she had taken pains to avoid him, ducking into classrooms when she saw him coming down the hall, staying out of his line of sight as much as was humanly possible. Without even looking up, he had indicated with his hand for her to sit down in the chair on the other side of his desk after she had knocked and come into his office that morning for the interview, and, with his eyes glued to the sheet of paper in front of him, he had said, "So, you're the daughter of Moishe Singer, the fruit man. Didn't we have a couple of your sisters here? How're they doing? Are they married yet?" Feigie could tell that Rabbi Berman didn't even remember her sisters' names. Then he looked up, stared at her as if he were probing her essence for an endless stretch of time, with his elbows planted on his desk and his bearded chin resting on a sling formed by his enlaced fingers and the bowl of his black velvet yarmulke tipped back exposing a half-moon of closely cropped gray hair, and finally, with his eyes still unyieldingly upon her, he had spoken. "So, tell me, Singer, what do you plan to do about those pimples of yours?" For fifteen minutes after that interview, she had sat on a toilet in one of the cubicles in the third-floor bathroom, her shoulders heaving, sobbing into her two hands pressed against her mouth. She could never imagine Rabbi Berman saying such a thing to Pessie or to Dvorah.

With God's help she could avoid him, she figured, at least until the second semester of her last year, when every graduating senior was required to take his course on the Laws of Family Purity. But that was a long time from now. Meanwhile she would try not to worry about it. And even then, when the time came, she could sit silently in a corner of the classroom, staring down into her lap. She would practice making herself transparent. He would not find her, he would not look for her. She was not interesting to him. This subject he taught, those laws, were what Pessie and Dvorah were discussing now. "The main point," Pessie said, "was that during those two weeks every month when you're not allowed to—you know—the main thing, like Berman said, is not to do anything to tempt your husband. Like, to excite him. Men are different that way—you know what I'm saying?" "Yeah," Dvorah responded, "but still you have to look good, even then. I mean, you still just can't get into bed with, like, cold cream or something smeared all over your face."

The two girls nodded. They were passing through a small clearing in the woods, and a shaft of light filtered down through the trees. Two squirrels ran out directly in their path, chasing each other, startling them. For the first time, Feigie remembered the animals that must inhabit these woods. Yet all this talk, this moment to which she was privileged, however frightening, however much her back and her legs hurt, this moment was stunning, like a revelation she could only partially comprehend. She listened as the two girls went on to analyze the significant members of their class, one by one, their looks and their personalities, their position in the group and their prospects, their good points and their bad, and then as they proceeded to scrutinize each other, commenting on each other's clothing and hairstyles, offering constructive criticism, touching lightly here and there to make a helpful point about possible improvements.

The conversation, in its way, was becoming more and more wonderful and deep to Feigie. And then it passed into a realm utterly mysterious, even fabulous. They began to speak in what, to Feigie's ears, sounded almost like a cryptic tongue, like secret knowledge from a hidden world. Their words struck her, each one discretely, like little pellets. "He called again last night," Dvorah reported to Pessie. "Yes, it was the same guy. For sure. The same voice. I'd recognize it anywhere. Yes, he said the same thing. The same thing in the same words. 'Tell your friend Pessie Glick that I'm going to kill her.' That's what he said. That he's going to kill you. It's really scary. And when I said to him, like you told me to, to call you up himself and tell you what he has against you, he just hung up. Like he always does. Just hung up."

Pessie turned coolly to face her friend. She said, "Well, as a matter of fact, he did call me last night finally, and we straightened the whole thing out, so he won't be bothering you anymore, Dvo."

"He called you? You're kidding! I don't believe it. That's really incredible." Dvorah's shock was alive in those woods, and dangerous, like a flash of lightning. Feigie could almost feel the current pass through those two superior girls, straight to her, to her, little Feigie Singer, to sear and to illuminate her, but she couldn't completely absorb it, it was too strong, she could not take it in, at least not then, she was feeling more and more sick, it was impossible to hide it from herself any longer. Her belly was tightening like a fist. The muscles in her thighs were pulled to a screech. The pain was breathtaking. She could see it as a separate entity in front of her. She needed to go off alone, to curl up like a wounded animal in a secluded place. She needed to be able to look at this thing. She could not continue. Most likely Pessie and Dvorah had never been struck so urgently, overwhelmed in such a mortifying, public way. She could not even picture them going to the bathroom. They seemed to be above all that. But she had to get some relief, and as the two girls immersed themselves ever deeper in their exotic language, Feigie slipped away and was lost.

She found a dark, mossy place within a heavy growth of trees. She set down her bag, slipped off her underpants, and crouched to the ground. She knew at once, with an ancient inborn knowledge, that something was different. With her fingers she felt the sticky warmth and wet. The smell was sweet and organic and intimate, hers. No one else could love it, she was sure. So it had come to her at last. It was the end. She knew its name, of course, from her sisters, she knew, yet she never truly expected it for herself. But it had befallen her nevertheless, as they claimed it befell all women, and now there was no longer any doubt that she would also, in the course of time, die. She had been sucked, whether she willed it or not, into the cycle. She took her little camera out of the plastic bag and pressed the flash. Her underwear was dark and soaked, she saw by the sharp snap of light, and her khaki skirt, when she flipped it back to front, was stained unmistakably. It was hopeless. Everyone would see. Pessie and Dvorah and Rabbi Berman— everyone. They would mock her. They would figure her out. She could not possibly go back now. She gathered some large flat leaves and placed them inside her underwear between her thighs. There was no escape. All choice had been taken from her. She could never leave the woods.

She waited for as long as she could bear to be safely lost, and then she rose and began to walk. She wanted to take out her prayer book and pray, but her hands were polluted from what she had just touched. First, she needed to find water. She had to wash, to purify herself. There were low signs stuck in the earth, she saw, painted with arrows. No, she would not follow them. She did not want to find her way out. But what if she came upon something, what if she came upon a man, say, prowling in this forest, what would she do then? What could she give to satisfy him? The money in her bag, her camera, her sandwich, the paltry jewels from her ears, her finger? She would grab the knife out of his hand. She would lay it across her hair and cut it all off. And she would give it to him. Her hair. She pulled the rubber band off her braid and slipped it around her wrist. She shook her hair loose, letting it fall free over her shoulders, down her back. But if it was an animal that came upon her in these woods, lured by the smell of her blood, what then? What would she have to give?

The pain gathered in intensity, it seemed almost loud, coming over her in great, constricting waves. It was tied to the blood. She passed a signpost emblazoned with arrows that seemed to be pointing skyward. She had never until now seen one like that. How could she possibly obey it, make the ascent, the sacrifice? Behind and alongside her as she advanced there was a rush of noise and movement. She began to climb in stiff long strides, not wanting to run, not wanting to show she was afraid, as she used to do when she was a child going down a long dark hallway, absolutely sure someone, something, a monster, was pursuing her, feeling it upon her back, draining her toward him. She was no longer a child. The strange sign appeared again, and then again, as if the creature trailing her in the shadows were picking it up as soon as she passed and running ahead to plant it at the next station, and then the next one, leading her to her destination, to the last of all possible signs, the sign that said, Enter.

She went inside. It was a cave. Here she would pass the night. She was hungry. She stretched out her hand, collected some leaves, squeezed and rubbed them in her palms, releasing the moisture. In this way she washed. She unwrapped her sandwich, taking a few bites, remembering to say the blessing before and after. Then she sealed it again in its foil and replaced it in her plastic bag, for later. She moved her lips in prayer, every chanted prayer by heart that could soothe her to sleep. A steady murmur and hum in the cave accompanied her prayers. Only when the full moon came up and cast a beam of light through the opening did she see who sang with her—a choir of snakes, tangled and snarled and intertwined in a kind of ecstasy. She ran out screaming. She was still lithe and spare—this might be the last time she could still run like a girl—she ran into the night and fell exhausted in the density of the forest, in a nest of pine needles and dead leaves.

When the dawn came up on the second day the woods seemed to be filling with men. She lay on her stomach under a thick blanket of forest droppings, alert, watching, her entire body concealed, only her eyes peering out, only the top of her hair visible, brown like the floor of these woods. A warm rain was falling. She emptied her plastic bag, stuffing the contents into her pockets, bit out three slits, for her eyes, her nose, and drew it over her head. They would never find her. What they would see, if they could see anything at all, would be litter, garbage, a discarded grocery sack. They would not see what was inside.

The pain, which had subsided in the night, began to mass once more. Between her legs there was a thickness, like paste. She bore down, struggled to push it out, strained to be delivered of this blood. Everywhere there were men, strange men, alien men from other worlds, worlds not her own, but also there were men she recognized, men in black hats, black coats, like brooding, great-winged birds. She watched them through the rain as they seemed to move entranced among the trees. What could such Jews be doing in these woods? Her Jews kept the sidewalks under their feet. Jews such as these—they gathered in forests only to be shot. Now and then, behind the rain, she imagined she heard them calling her name—Feigie, Feigie. But how could that be? Then she understood. These were the ones they called the Dead Hasidim, the enraptured ones who sought solitude in nature to commune with God. They were calling in Yiddish to the birds.

All day she watched them through the slits of her plastic bag, her body underground, the rain falling steadily. She felt herself beginning to be cleansed. Af-Bri was the name of the angel of rain. That was what Rabbi Berman had told them at an assembly early in the school year, around the time you say the Prayer for Rain. *Af* for anger, rain that pours down in torrents and floods; *Bri* for health, sweet rain that refreshes and renews. For life and not for death—those were the words you chanted at the end of the prayer. "Remember that, girls," Rabbi Berman had said, "life, not death." Up there alone on that stage he looked for a moment almost like some mother's child. She could pity him.

When it was nearly dark, the woods emptied out. The rain had ended. Feigie took the plastic bag off her head and, like one who had passed through a grave sickness, shook off the earth that had covered her and rose. She began to walk among the trees, the wet ground giving under her feet. She gazed down at herself as she walked, and she thought, I am transformed, no one will recognize me.

She walked until the moon came out, until she found the cradle of the dead oak hollowed out for her. This is where she would remain. She climbed inside and curled up into herself against the cold, one arm underneath her body supporting her head, the other across her chest, the palm of her hand resting over her heart, stroking her breast. She did not know if this was allowed. In this way she fell asleep.

At dawn she awoke with her heart pounding, launched out of a dream of wolves and bears. She stood up in terror inside the shell of her dead tree. A black dog froze in place, its cold eyes upon her. Who is a Jew? The one with the inborn fear of dogs. Three men in the distance started and turned sharply. In the early morning light, she could see that each man was carrying a long weapon in his hands. Hunters. They were moving toward her. They had seen her. Nothing remained but surrender. As the groom draws closer to lift the veil over her face, the most pious of brides does not raise her eyes to look but keeps them cast down. She prays. Feigie sat down inside her cradle and took out her prayer book. She never lifted her eyes. Desperately, she prayed. Like a bride.

Forbidden City

When the Gobi Desert came to Beijing on the first day of the lunar month, Reb Pesach Tikkun-Olam Salzman, known throughout China as the Zaddik of Sin for his celebrated deeds of righteousness, told his girls to get up and put on their masks—they would grab this opportunity for an outing to the Forbidden City to sing morning prayers. True, the sands of the wasteland had been advancing toward the capital for years now, borne in on savage winds meeting weaker and weaker resistance as the Bosses set about taking down all nonessential barriers standing in the path of expansion and progress. Reb Tikkun-Olam, by the way, was in full agreement with the Bosses on this policy, as he found himself to be on almost every other issue. "What for do we need trees anyway?" Reb Tikkun-Olam would say. "Who ever heard of a normal human being having a vision sitting up in a tree? But in the desert—ah, that's another story entirely. There's no such thing as too much desert."

In fact, he and the Bosses were partners, collaborators in the most constructive sense of the word; quietly and behind the scenes they did business together, especially in matters pertaining to the acquisition and distribution of the girls. They were like the assembly of seventy-one sages in ancient Israel, Reb Tikkun-Olam liked to say of the Bosses, perplexing the official with whom he was haggling concerning final arrangements re one of the girls—"Like the Sanhedrin of old," Reb Tikkun-Olam would make a stab at clarifying, "you know, the *Sin*-hedrin, so to speak," he would add with a throwaway laugh like a shrug. The fact that the Hebrew word for China was *Sin* was a sly message that Reb Tikkun-Olam took benign delight in communicating, particularly to an agent of the Bosses who was trying to squeeze every last cent out of him on a deal involving the girls, and whose English was good enough to get the point without taking undue offense. As for the girls themselves, one of their selling points was that they all knew English, it was a prerequisite for an American market, they were bilingual in comprehension even if they could not speak at all by the time he was finished with them; the language germ was carefully implanted, he guaranteed this in writing.

In the mornings, wrapped in his prayer shawl and bound in his phylacteries, with his girls, those who were able to stand on their own two feet lined up in order behind a bamboo screen as he led them in the Benedictions and intoned his gratitude to the Lord, *For not having made me a woman*, he gave them the choice of either the traditional feminine substitution, *For having made me according to His will*, or alternatively, an original neuter variant of his own spawning, *For having made me Sin-i*—that's how much Reb Tikkun-Olam respected the Chinese. No question, Reb Tikkun-Olam had a deep and abiding regard for the Chinese—deep and abiding, he would reiterate. The Chinese were, in his personal opinion, a mutant form of Jew—hardworking, high IQs, possessing a genetic gift for mathematics, business, music, with a specialty in string instruments, and so on, clumping right there with the Jews along the superior tail of the bell, and, of course, also like the Jews, they were a minimum of five thousand years old and long-suffering. The main difference, Reb Tikkun-Olam liked to say, was that there were a whole lot of them, whereas, on the other hand, not so many of us. Despite God's promise to Abraham, Reb Tikkun-Olam commented, it was they, and not us, who were so multitudinous that they could not be counted—like the sands of the Gobi now coming to bury Beijing. With his girls, at least this situation of the disparity in numbers was something that the Zaddik of Sin, in his own small way, was doing his part to correct.

Why Reb Tikkun-Olam was inspired on this day of all days to treat his girls to a field trip was that the sand was pouring down so thickly, like a cascading drapery of bone scrim behind which nothing but flailing shadows were visible, that it created, in his estimation, an ideal environment in terms of protecting his girls from prying eyes, sparing them from unwanted attention. Not only they but everyone without exception would be wearing a mask that day, his girls would not stand out, and, also, of course, there was the sensitive issue of modesty. Reb Tikkun-Olam stressed modesty; it was a subject about which he was known to be ultra strict. Even within the walls of their rooms in their small dwelling in the narrow, winding *hutong* in the heart of Beijing, Reb Tikkun-Olam required that his girls be fully covered at all times. Only their small pale hands showed from the wrists fanning out. Every strand of silken black hair, plus the dark orifices and tender, pendulous flesh of the ears, were concealed under a blue cotton kerchief, though indoors, for health considerations and to ease problems related to breathing and speech, and of course, for taking in essential nutrients, Reb Tikkun-Olam permitted the girls to be without the mask that straddled the bump of the nose, the moistness of the nostrils, and most importantly, the red wound of the mouth, which, in Reb Tikkun-Olam's opinion, was a far more intimate zone than, let us say, the hair, although, according to traditional classifications, the hair ranked third in the levels of female nakedness after, first, the frank nakedness of the body from the neck down and second, the nakedness of the woman's voice, whereas for some unfathomable reason, the mouth itself from which the voice emanated did not rank at all—an omission that never failed to set Reb Tikkun-Olam's head shaking back and forth in bemusement, it was so manifestly naive.

However, needless to say, if the girls ventured out into the *hutong* courtyard for even one second to fulfill some purpose or other, they were obliged to put on their masks, no exemptions granted. But this happened very seldom; after all there was plenty to keep them pleasantly occupied right inside the house at all times, what with the sands of the Gobi Desert penetrating day after day through the cracks in the walls, or even through the door and windows if, from lack of consideration, some guilty party failed to seal them shut promptly. Just a few spoons and cups, maybe a sieve or a funnel or a colander, perhaps a small pot or pan—that was all that was required to keep the girls busy indoors. For hours they would squat there on the floor, their feet tucked compactly under their haunches, playing within their own four cubits in perfect contentment, constructing imaginary cities of pavilions and palaces and pathways in their own private sandbox.

The one charged with the task of sweeping up the sand into piles and carrying out other assorted housekeeping chores, plus tending and supervising the girls, not to mention performing such services for Reb Tikkun-Olam himself as picking the grains of sand out of the crevices and creases, folds and furrows of his soft, large body, was Dolly, the name instantly bestowed upon her by Reb Tikkun-Olam's youngest daughter just a short while before his wife Frumie declared that she couldn't take it anymore and headed straight back to her parents' house in Brooklyn with all eight of their kids. Until it had been her peculiar fate to land in Beijing, the Rebbetzin Frumie Salzman had known absolutely nothing of the Chinese except the laundries on Bedford Avenue, where she used to bring her husband's white shirts for heavy starch, and twice a year, around the Yom Kippur and Passover holidays, his long white *kittel*. Even the restaurants meant zero to her, she never noticed them at all on the streets at home since they had no connection whatsoever to her life, some wise guy once told her that they didn't mix meat with milk in there, which was the lame excuse, she figured, for why a certain category of so-called Jews considered it a commandment of their faith to eat Chinese at least once a week—but she herself was strictly kosher, super glatt, what are you talking about? And chopsticks? Don't even get me started on chopsticks, Frumie cried. What was China to her? Dishes—five-piece place settings displayed in a blond-veneered breakfront next to the sterling and cut crystal—that's all she ever needed or wanted to know about China, anything else was more information than she could bear, thank you very much. Oh, why were they ever shipped off to be Judaism's emissaries in such a strange land, an assignment to the opposite end of the earth, to where she used to pretend to dig in the dirt as a little girl but never truly hoped to arrive, it was like another planet, with only a handful of local Jewish remnants in any halfway recognizable shape or form targeted for outreach, but no matter how much you knocked yourself out to draw them in it was hopeless, they were already such a lost cause, it was a total waste of energy, and other than these miserable specimens, nothing but Jewish tourists passing through, flatulent tourists on packages to whom she in her wig and her husband in his black hat and beard were an in-joke, familiar freaks, a couple of snapped curiosities in an album, or for the more nostalgic among them, a comforting taste of home, like the Jewish McDonalds. China was exile, China was punishment. What had she done to deserve it? By the waters of Babylon there we sat and also we wept as we remembered Zion. What in the world was China doing alongside Mount Sinai?

It was because the child resembled a tiny porcelain doll that the name had stuck when Reb Tikkun-Olam brought Dolly home that day, more than ten years earlier. He had found her sitting solitary, absolutely alone, absolutely still and expressionless like a baby Buddha on a torn and filthy straw mat with a tin can for coins stinking of fish placed beside her and flies swarming around her head on Wangfujing Street in front of a department store. "Just what we needed," Frumie said as the entire family gathered around and Reb Tikkun-Olam peeled off her soiled rags to confirm their assumption with regard to the gender; the Chinese, they knew very well, even the most desperate, did not just leave their precious boys lying around in the street like stray dogs for any stranger to pick up. The girl lay totally unresisting as they closed in to inspect her, her eyes frozen, never letting out the faintest cry. Reb Tikkun-Olam used the occasion to instruct his children in the lesson that the first piece of information sought out about a human being, at the moment of birth, is derived from a swift glance to the private parts; it is in that direction that the eyes of all present automatically turn and this is the first news that is reported before any other, this is the screaming headline. And afterward, too, Reb Tikkun-Olam taught, what is always noted and registered first when you meet a new person, imperceptibly, whether you realize it or not, before any other business is commenced, is the sex, gleaned from the visible secondary characteristics, you tick off a little box inside your brain—male or female or other or whatever—so you will know how to proceed, which was another reason, Reb Tikkun-Olam pointed out, always to be on guard to practice the strictures of modesty—defensively, like a shield, like a suit of armor to protect you against the intrusiveness of such scrutiny.

Dolly was maybe between one and three years old, they estimated, when Reb Tikkun-Olam found her and carried her home under his arm like the baby lamb from the market that father bought; it was impossible to know her age exactly, she was so small, yet fully formed, with the defined shape and gravity of a resigned mortal. She was strangely passive and robotic for a child, which at first led Reb Tikkun-Olam to conjecture that she might have been massively drugged before being set out there in the street to beg for the family, but when she continued to maintain that odd impenetrable composure, and, moreover, practically every single one of the many girls he had processed since that time over the subsequent years also demonstrated some variation of a similar blankness, Reb Tik-kun-Olam decided that this must simply be how it was—this was an ethnic type, there was no point in arguing with nature, perhaps God in His wisdom created them that way for a very good purpose, innately obedient and submissive for survival reasons, a definite market value could be set on such qualities, especially for a woman. For his part, he, the Zaddik of Sin, would receive them as they were, he would not seek to change them, he would love them unconditionally, he would sanctify his energies to labor on their behalf.

When Reb Tikkun-Olam announced that he believed that the child had been sent to him by God to show him his mission on earth, Frumie registered silently that this was it; the time had come to call her mother and start packing. It was also around then that he declared he would no longer answer to the name Pesach, given to him by his father to mark his arrival on Passover eve, his exemplary mother taking only the necessary time off from the strenuous preparations for the holiday to give birth to him—it all went very quickly, he was her fourteenth child—smoothing her housecoat and getting up to resume her work in time to roast the shankbone and grate the bitter herbs. Henceforth, he advised Frumie, he would be known as Tikkun-Olam, to denote his kabbalistic mandate to repair the shattered vessels of this world.

It had not escaped Frumie's notice that he had become pro-gressively weirder and weirder, in her opinion, as the years accumulated in this upside-down place China. For example, instead of dressing like a normal person, in a black kaftan with a tasseled rope belt to separate the lower, carnal section of his body from the upper, spiritual part, and a fringed garment as a reminder that he belongs to the One Above, a black hat on weekdays in all seasons over his velvet yarmulke and a sleek fur *streimel* on the Sabbath, he now decked himself out bizarrely in a long embroidered turquoise silk Chinese robe, loose drawstring pants that required pulling down to do all his business, cotton shoes like a mourner, and on his head a black satin skullcap with a ridiculous pompom; he looked like a Confucius with side curls, it was understandably very embarrassing to introduce him on those rare occasions when friends or family took the trouble to trek around the globe to visit. And even more upsetting, something she was too ashamed to confide to another soul, even to her own mother, was the period of time during which he would not stop badgering her to organize a *rosh hodesh* prayer group exclusively for women, it was her responsibility as his helpmeet to undertake this project, he insisted, he was envisioning a women's celebration to welcome in the new moon at the head of each month through ritual that harnessed the natural female lunar energy, he said, with chants and dances, and an altar and candles and incense and a vessel to collect the cyclic blood.

But the last straw for Frumie came when he informed her that although all the other discarded girls he would be rescuing as part of his mission to repair the world would be for the purpose of finding them good Jewish homes and adoptive Jewish parents from among the increasing numbers of older overeducated infertile Jewish couples of America with dual incomes who could afford the fees, thereby, as a side benefit of saving the children, also drawing from the demographic plenitude and genetic variation of the Chinese to correct the population shortage and chronic inbreeding among the Jews, throwing in as a bonus the extra service of personally converting the girls in advance through ritual-bath immersion, like pre-koshered chickens, already salted and soaked—this particular girl, this Dolly, his first, he would keep, not for his own sake, God forbid, but for hers, for Frumie's sake, to raise Dolly to serve as his *pilegesh* when she came of age so that he would no longer have to bother Frumie with his needs even during the periods when she was not ritually impure, when she was technically available to him, albeit suffering from a terrible migraine. Though the revered medieval scholar and physician Maimonides had decreed that a concubine is permissible only to a king, other rabbinical authorities have argued that to preserve peace in the household between husband and wife, and to offset the masculine tendency to fool around either with oneself or with others if not satisfactorily serviced, an appreciative *pilegesh* was indeed a practical solution, which, in the end, did not really hurt anyone. Never mind the Old Testament account of the *pilegesh* from Gibeah, handed over to the gang to be molested, and then butchered and hacked up into twelve parcels and sent special delivery to each of the tribes of Israel as a cautionary message regarding property rights. That happened very long ago, in the wild east of the Judges; it was ancient history, it was no longer relevant. These, on the other hand, were modern times, Reb Tikkun-Olam pointed out, enlightened times, and China was the country of the future—China was the cutting edge.

Pushing with his troop of girls through the heavy gauze of the swirling sand to the Forbidden City, Reb Tikkun-Olam was thinking, This must be it, the approaching day that is neither day nor night, as the prophet had foreseen. Ungraspable apocalyptic shades were thrashing in the miasma in front of them as their little procession lunged ahead. Lashing blindly with weapons choked with grit, a phalanx of guards posted by the Bosses sought in vain to seize the lone Falun Dafa practitioner in defiant slow motion, taunting them behind the screen of raining sand in the vast desert that had once been Tiananmen Square. Reb Tikkun-Olam trudged behind his girls through this end-of-the-world landscape, clutching the tail of the rope that linked them all in one line. Instead of a mask, his capacious white prayer shawl with the licorice-black stripes and the neck ornamentation of silver and gold embroidery was drawn across the lower portion of his face and hooded over the phylactery box on his head—like a Bedouin in a sandstorm, he pictured himself, Salzman of Arabia.

Dolly, too, at the head of the line, with her end of the rope looped around her wrist, was also excused from wearing a mask. This was because her slight form, showing only the barest, though unmistakable, suggestions of budding womanhood, was shrouded from the top of her head to the tips of her toes in a stale bedsheet, which had been fashioned like a burka, the perfect garment for what turned out, after all, to be a classical Islamic climate—Reb Tikkun-Olam could only marvel at the way practical and spiritual imperatives merged in the costumes of evolving cultures. Over the narrow rectangular opening cut out for her eyes, thick tinted glasses in black plastic frames were perched, which they obtained free of charge through the good offices of the Bosses and renewed annually as her eyesight progressively deteriorated. A short while after he had carried Dolly home, and Frumie absconded with the kids, it became clear that the explanation for the hours during which the girl would lie mute, curled up under the table with eyes stubbornly shut, was not attributable to incipient brattiness or plain ingratitude, say, or to infantile depression, as some visiting American woman magazine-reader had insinuated, but rather, was actually due to a concrete problem—the child had difficulty seeing and had simply given up trying.

It was then that Reb Tikkun-Olam was struck with his second revelation regarding his new mission: not only would he rescue the Chinese girl babies dumped out by families who would accept nothing less than a boy for the one-child-per policy strictly mandated by the Bosses to stanch the population glut, but his niche would be placing for adoption the problem cases—seconds, irregulars, damaged goods, so to speak—Specials, as Reb Tikkun-Olam labeled them to shoppers, because, first of all, they were "special" in the euphemistic sense, and secondly, he could also offer them at a special price, a nice discount, cut-rate, cheap, relatively speaking—ultimately making up the difference in volume. And to his gratification, in his targeted US markets, from Cambridge, Massachusetts, to New York City's Upper West Side to Berkeley, California, for example, prospective clients responded overwhelmingly, leaping with ferocious energy and resourcefulness to claim these markdowns. Not only did they perversely prefer girls, Reb Tikkun-Olam was stunned to discover, and not only did they favor Chinese girls who would inevitably be italicized among all those Semitic types in the Byzantine world of girlhood intrigue, but astonishingly, counterintuitively, they prized the added challenges, as they called them, the bonus disabilities, physical and/or mental, that came with Reb Tikkun-Olam's particular stock, which would be overcome by their professional competence and their mastery of detail and their genius for follow-up, their lists and schedules, their contacts and connections, they never doubted their powers for a minute. There was no joke that God could possibly perpetrate through His infinite and grotesque variations on a theme that could faze them; Reb Tikkun-Olam was awed and humbled. In spite of all the evidence to the contrary, they believed with a full faith that they were in control.

The three infants, to take a case in point, that Dolly in her ghostly robe was now carrying in the soft hammock-like sling across her almost but not quite flat chest, would be snatched up by these customers within the year—Reb Tikkun-Olam had absolutely no worries on that score; the profit margin would be satisfactory, there were no anticipated problems with overstock or remainders. They had been delivered just the previous week by the Bosses, deposited at dawn in a suitcase at their doorstep in the *hutong*. When he opened the suitcase he actually found five girl babies packed inside, but two, not surprisingly, had already spoiled, and had to be picked out, like moldy strawberries at the bottom of the basket, and set out by the side of the road to be collected for recycling. Of the three that remained, now being borne by Dolly in her improvised baby tote like fledgling doves to the Forbidden City, one's feet were crippled, maybe from botched binding, the second had a dark port wine stain on her cheek in a shape that resembled a cartoon dragon, and while the third had no obvious defect or deformity, Reb Tikkun-Olam never questioned for a moment that there was something wrong with her—the Bosses never made a mistake in these early detection matters, probably it was some kind of mental issue, a self-esteem problem, maybe, or a suicidal tendency, not yet discernible to the naked eye but diagnosed by wise men who placed three fingers on the pulse and consulted the charts.

As usual, all of the girls were called Lily. When he first started in business, he would give each one her own individual name, giving himself a headache at the same time as he struggled to come up with something perfect and unique to match the face pictured in the catalogue and the website blurbs. But what was the point of going to all that trouble, after all? At that age, you could hardly tell them apart anyway. And should he need to summon or refer to one of them, it didn't really matter in the end which one it was; any one of them would do just as well as another. Besides, as soon as the deal was finalized and ownership transferred, a personalized name would be bestowed by the adoptive family upon its new daughter—Shoshana-Bracha Mei-Ling Srulovich-Seltzer, or another such equally creative effort; the name pool was open and available and free for anyone to dip into. In the meantime, for the sake of efficiency, instead of names, prospective customers could refer to the desired item by noting the catalogue number within the lily logo underneath the mug shot. The Lilys that Dolly was transporting in her pouch through the Gobi wind and sand that morning were numbers 394 through 396. Five Lilys, Lily number 311 through Lily 315, were plodding in a row behind her along the extended rope, which was noosed around each of their waists in turn and culminated in Reb Tikkun-Olam's fist.

These five, as it happened, were proving to be an extremely difficult lot to place; Reb Tikkun-Olam would definitely incur a severe loss due to them especially when you factored in the maintenance expenses and overhead costs for well over the year that they had already been with him. What rendered them almost unmarketable as a product, so to speak, was that, in addition to their other problems, they were afflicted with the one drawback that even Reb Tikkun-Olam's usual clientele, with all their managerial expertise and enthusiasm, could do nothing to overcome—namely, their age. They were appealingly miniature, true, but nevertheless there was no getting around the fact that they were already well past the optimal age for adoption, like expired merchandise in a grocery case, which, in the end, could only be tossed out. Reb Tikkun-Olam suspected that three of them at least might even already be in the two-digit range, from which, once entered in a lifetime, there is, except in the rarest of cases, no exit. They had been deposited on his doorstep in a plastic dumpster marked Guangdong Province Hospital, huddling on a bed of blood and pus-stained bandages and other assorted medical waste. It was essentially for the sake of these overage five that all of them were struggling that morning to part the heavy curtains of sand and make their way to pray in the Forbidden City, which Reb Tikkun-Olam regarded as a holy place, especially for women, by virtue of its sediments of concentrated unrecorded ancient female suffering, both inflicted and endured. Hearing their prayers from this sacred site, perhaps the Master of the Universe would look upon these foundlings with kindness and arrange suitable homes for them at last, as He has been known to occasionally turn a mischievous prankster's eye upon some ill-favored woman as she prayed for a husband—nothing fancy, just any old husband, please God—and grant her wish. They were dressed in faded-blue Mao suits too large for them, these five Lily rejects, and blue cotton kerchiefs wound tightly around their lowered heads. Naturally, in strict adherence to the rules, they all wore their masks.

Bringing up the rear of his file of girls, Reb Tikkun-Olam responded to the automatic bow of the ticket collector at the entrance gate to the Forbidden City with a jaunty salute of his own patent, taking care to give no sign whatsoever that could in any way be interpreted as bowing in return. A Jew bows down only to the One Above, for this gentile's information; for that principle alone the throats of centuries of martyrs had been cut. Despite the custom of the land, not even with the slightest dip of the head would Reb Tikkun-Olam allow himself to betray his holy ancestors—the Chinese, even these atheist officials, appreciated a man who respected his ancestors—and certainly he would never execute any facsimile of the prostration and the banging of the brow on the stones that was the throbbing pulse within the walls and moats of this compound in imperial days, he could feel the vibration of the head-pounding rising up still from the tortured ground. By prior arrangement with the Bosses, the ticket collector waved them through, compliments of the house—the least you could expect, really, when you considered the percentage cut that Reb Tikkun-Olam was obliged to fork over for the Bosses' cooperation on every single deal he closed involving the girls. The little smirk on the ticket collector's face at the spectacle of this oversized alien gone native wrapped in some kind of white horse blanket with a black leather cube strapped to his head, and his menagerie of harnessed girls in tow, blindered and muzzled, was a fact of life that Reb Tikkun-Olam had grown immunized to over the years in Beijing. On the one hand, it was an insult and condescension he might coldly ignore, as no doubt was warranted, but on the other hand, it was important to be on friendly terms with the locals, and especially with the officials linked to the Bosses, so in man-to-man code to this ticket collector, Reb Tikkun-Olam gave a rough yank to his end of the rein as he drove his team through the Gate of Supreme Harmony, tipping his line of girls precariously backward in the stinging sand, and with his free arm lashing in the Gobi wind, he mimicked the rise and fall of a whip's arc.

The point was to get his girls as efficiently as possible past the great public ceremonial spaces with their wooden palaces and halls in glossy reds and golds—the aesthetic prototype, in Reb Tikkun-Olam's mind, for Chinese restaurants in malls across America, a genre of establishment that, to be perfectly honest, he had entered only once in his lifetime in a bathroom emergency and was nearly wiped out by an alien smell, probably pork. He hustled his girls forward through the sand-streaked atmosphere, past dogged tourists persevering in the face of mounting panic as the relentlessly falling grit stuffed up every hole in their equipment, past the sand-plugged bronze incense burners and great water urns that eunuch slaves kept filled day and night to prevent the place from burning to the ground.

Wherever Reb Tikkun-Olam turned, peasants were invading the palaces. Cutting his way through the masses, he steered his charges toward the private inner courtyards of the gynaeceum at the northern end of the complex. Maybe they would hold their prayer service in the Hall of Forgotten Favorites, he was thinking, that might be appropriate, but he had not yet made a final decision. Because setting aside all of the evidence pressing in upon them from every corner, of idol worship, of debauchery, of extravagance, of intrigue, what was this place after all but a retirement home for used concubines? And all things considered, it was not such a bad deal for some nice Mongol debutante from a decent family, Reb Tikkun-Olam reflected—a lifetime pension, including room and board and a whole array of perks within the confines of this five-star estate for what might amount in the end to less than a single night's work if you weren't overly ambitious—express delivery, gift-wrapped in a black cloak, over the spongy shoulder of a royal eunuch, offloaded on the floor at the foot of the dynastic bed, bathed and perfumed and depilated and stripped naked as a security precaution against the concealed dagger you might plunge into the heart of the Son of Heaven. Was one night's work too much to expect in exchange for guaranteed tenure in this exclusive domain, with all of its comforts and luxuries, Reb Tikkun-Olam asked himself as he pushed ahead in the spectral landscape toward the Imperial Garden.

Through the veils of sand he could barely make out the slumped backs of his leftover girls straining along the rope emanating from him like his own entrails unraveling. Searching for the fading vision of Dolly at the head of the line, his eyes were guided downward along her body, coming to rest at a startling burst of crimson stain radiating through the haze of sand and grit from her pale robe where it tented out ever so subtly. So it has come to her at last, Reb Tikkun-Olam took in—a significant moment, a milestone, a life-cycle event. He understood that she might now be too drained to walk all the way home after the service, though naturally she would never raise her voice to utter a word of complaint; he might have to carry her, though, along with the spared newborns in her sack, as he had carried her on the day she was found, when she was also unclean. And then, once they were home, once she had removed her street garment and taken off her glasses, it would be his duty to strike her, yes, he would be obliged to slap her on the face—an old custom at the onset of womanhood, mysterious, or more precisely, mystical, yet necessary. And Dolly had no mother to do it for her, poor child.

The lustful mothers of China, the dragon ladies, Dowager Empress Cixi and Madame Mao, liked to do something nice for themselves on the first day of the lunar month, taking a well-deserved break from their posts behind the bamboo screen where they painstakingly fed words into the mouths of the enthroned Son of Heaven and the Chairman giving audience on the other side, accompanied by a sisterhood of concubines whom they had handpicked to nourish the male energy, personally rating each beauty contestant for a discreet Adam's apple and regular teeth and pink tongue and sweet breath and plump uvula; on these days they were borne on palanquins by fat eunuchs through the Imperial Garden of the Forbidden City up the fourteen meters along winding pathways to the top of the Hill of Accumulated Refinement for the empowering refreshment and relaxation of enjoying the view. The view, Reb Tikkun-Olam noted, as far as the eye could see, was sand blowing, flying, twisting wildly on agitated currents of air. The civilizing divisions between heaven and earth laid down during the first days of creation bringing order to the world had vanished entirely. The spirit of the Gobi was churning over the face of the waters.

Reb Tikkun-Olam, now at the head of the line, jerked the rope urgently, dragging his girls up the hill into the shelter of the pavilion at the top. Sand was falling all over China. The Forbidden City below, and everything that lay beyond, was returning to dust. From the viewing pavilion at the top of the Hill of Accumulated Refinement they could see nothing, emptiness and void, nor could they be seen in turn. It would be safe now for his five girls yoked along the rope to lower their masks. When they opened their mouths for prayer, their raw harelips and their cleft palates would not offend. The shredded sounds coiling upward from their mouths, rising in lamentation, would not violate the strictures of modesty as he was the only male present to hear their naked voices—and he was like a father to them. Their naked voices would be covered by the voice of the Lord causing the desert to tremble.

Reb Tikkun-Olam removed his phylacteries in anticipation of the additional service commemorating the head of the month sacrifices on the altars of the holy temple, destroyed for our sins. It was essential that they block out all earthly distractions, focus inward spiritually, concentrate intensely. Maybe God would incline favorably toward them and be appeased, maybe He would accept their prayers in lieu of the new-moon burnt offerings—the pair of bulls, the ram, and the young lambs, unblemished.

The Plot

When Luba Popkin flushed, Lola Blitzer's pipes shuddered—an awful intimacy, the spasm of personal water shunting downward through her walls, a disturbance almost every hour of every night lately, not that Lola herself really slept that much anymore either. Luba's swollen feet across Lola's ceiling all night long, plodding from bed to toilet, crashing into objects, the downpour of her nightly shower to calm herself, trick herself into sleep, the throbbing of her television going full time to keep her company in her widowhood when she was in, a precaution against robbers when she was out—Lola knew entirely too much about this stranger, Luba Popkin, due to the accident of living stacked up on each other. It was so unseemly. For thirty years, maybe longer, they nodded in formal recognition if by chance they crossed paths entering or leaving their building on Amsterdam Avenue, or happened to be downstairs at the same time, when the postman delivered the Social Security checks, and also, it goes without saying, when they met by the garbage. But it was not until Lola volunteered to join the neighborhood women's hevra kadisha bereavement committee that they were officially introduced, when she was partnered with Luba, already a pro in the tahara rituals of purification and preparation of a dead body for burial, and the two of them took their places side by side in front of the corpse.

She was a heavy woman in her early sixties, a quarter century younger by a rough estimate than either Lola or Luba, a contemporary, give or take, of the other two women working alongside them, the entire holy society purification team safely within the postmenstrual decontaminated finish line and though they had been forewarned by one of the directors of the funeral home, they were obliged to silently beg her forgiveness for transgressing the dignity of the dead by inwardly recoiling when she was unwrapped. It wasn't just the pits of knotted scarring where the breasts had been, or the long pale gash in the waxy flesh of the lower belly, in the region of the womb, or the sparse wisps of coiled hair where the legs forked and on the head, or the bruises on elbows and knees—this lady was a faller, Lola recognized the type at once, Lola's mother had been a faller too—it wasn't even the toothless mouth gaping rigidly open, like the mouths of those wretched souls Lola used to see when she still rode the subways, drooping helplessly into calamitous sleep late at night, like dogs, like her mother's mouth the night Lola had been ordered to sit guard in the slow-motion first moments afterward, while adult arrangements were being made, the family secret of the inside of her mother's mouth was more than she could bear, she was nine years old, she had tried to prop it closed by wedging a book under the jaw, slamming that mouth shut with an upward thrust of the book, a big book, her mother's favorite, a cautionary tale, *Anna Karenina*, but the minute they marched back in they yanked it out in horror, and the jaw fell slack down again. In that brief glimpse of the entire body, when the corpse was exposed for the first time, in the few seconds before a clean sheet could be stretched across it for modesty and respect, there was the humiliating spectacle of the open mouth, yes, but more hopeless than that, to Lola's mind, was the nail polish, assiduously applied on all ten fingers and toes, just a day or two ago at most, living color. Her mother's fingernails were lacquered too, oxygenated red, to match her lipstick exactly. There was nothing Lola ever knew more minutely in her entire life than her mother's hands, the flat wart pressing against the rubbed gold wedding ring, the rough-knuckled thumb and thick forefinger stretched glossy and taut to pincer the metallic tube as she leaned forward to the mirror to put on her outside face— the gelatinous red scrawl across the lips, the clown stain on the tissue, the sharp, stale, spit odor rising—Lola would stand there silently, gazing upward, observing closely. Her mother was not thinking about her. Lola had been ruined forever by her mother's unhappiness.

Removing the nail polish, that was the first job Luba assigned her, and also the hospital bracelet. Sherry something was the name of this woman who had once dealt with this body full time, who alone privately savored inhaling its smells. Decay was in the air, sweet creamy liquefaction, maggots and worms already breeding wildly, it was futile to struggle against them, Lola knew this firsthand from her late-life career as a boutique picker of lice and nits from the golden heads of the children of the rich. Discreetly, Lola sucked in her breath as she toiled to block out the odor of putrefaction that was growing more and more insistent; she dimmed her eyes against the fishy blueness and bloating of the corpse, she numbed her touch to the parchment-brittle skin and alien coldness as she cleaned under the nails with a toothpick, prying open the clawed fingers to reveal a petrified Kleenex—another charter member of the society of tissue-clutching women, Lola noted, as she was herself, and yes, her mother too; this tissue fossil must be placed inside the coffin and buried with her, Lola was informed, there were bloodstains on it, it was a body part. Lola penetrated the ears with a Q-tip, the nostrils, and so on, combing, grooming, while Luba, along with the other two women, washed the body with lukewarm water, first the front, uncovering only the designated part as they worked on it, inclining it on the left side, then on the right, to do the back, chanting all the while lines from the sacred love song. Your eyes like doves, Your cheeks, Your lips, Your arms, Your thighs. Then Luba alone, still strong as an ox in her ninth decade of life and weighing in at over two hundred and twenty pounds, stood Sherry on the floor and held her upright while the others poured three eight-quart buckets of water totaling nine *kavim* over her head in a continuous flow to stream down her body, chanting, She is pure, She is pure, She is pure, in accordance with the verse, And I will throw pure water on you and you will be purified, from all of your impurities and from all of your abominations I will purify you. Sweat pooling in their armpits and leaking down their sides, breathing heavily, they raised her leaden limbs to dress her in priestly white linen shrouds, the blouse, the robe without pockets to certify to security that she was passing through unarmed, arching her hips upward to draw the trousers over the meat of belly and buttocks, the sash pleated to form the pitchforked *shin* of the merciful divine's name, the cap. Ministering to the dead was regarded as the noblest of all acts of loving-kindness because no earthly gratitude from the recipient could be expected—that's what Lola had been taught during the orientation, but when they finally settled Sherry into her plain pine coffin and quit bothering her at last, there was an audible deflation as she relaxed into place, an audible sigh of relief not to be handled ever again, to be left alone finally—they all heard it, Thank you, Thank you. They shut her mouth once and for all by stuffing it with a clean white rag, a cloth was stretched over the face to veil her for eternity, she was mummified in a white sheet, shards of earthenware from the holy land and the dust to which she was already returning were strewn over the eyes, the mouth, the heart, the genitals. Sherry, daughter of Irwin, they addressed her, we ask your forgiveness if in any way we have dishonored you, we were just doing our jobs according to our tradition. When they do me, Lola made a mental note, they'll use my mother's name—Lola daughter of Golda—I'll get Luba to make sure.

Which was why, after they adjusted the lid on top of the coffin and washed their hands and stepped outside, stricken by the indifferent light of day, instead of hurrying home in accordance with her established personal policy of paring away all attachments, animate and inanimate, Lola lingered in front of the funeral home alongside Luba. She had quite lost whatever little talent she might once have possessed at making friends, or, even more degrading, at asking a favor for herself—how did a person go about it anyway?—and the thought of giving off the suspicion that she might be lonely, needy, was appalling. Still, it might not appear too pathetic to stick to Luba for a respectable interval and wait for a sign; they were pointed in the same direction after all, home was in the same building, there was an explanation, an excuse. Two old ladies propped up against the backdrop of a funeral parlor—who would pay attention anyway?—and she, Lola, so austere and miniature, under five feet tall now and shrinking steadily, parked alongside this monumental Luba, topped off with her lavender pouf hairdo. Such a ridiculous couple they must have been, Lola was just picturing it through the indecent eyes of a stranger from every demeaning angle when Luba took her elbow and steered her down the street. "So you come mit me now to the Utopia for a bite to eat maybe? I always have a little nosh after I do one—a little present to me, myself, and I—to remind me that Luba Popkin, she ain't dead yet."

In the coffee shop, jammed into the booth across from Luba, sipping her tea from the heavy varicosed cup that had been pressed between generations of all varieties of sinful lips, Lola observed as her companion dug shamelessly into her chunk of quivering meringue, washing it all down with hot chocolate—"mit extra *schlag*, LaToya darling," she had specified to the waitress, who rolled her eyes and nodded, obviously trained to Luba's preferences. "You eat for the birds," Luba commented to Lola. "Me, I was always a good eater, thanks God, I was always a big girl. Strong. That's what saved me from the showers." She pushed up her left sleeve to show off the fading blue numbers tattooed onto the loosening mottled skin of her forearm. "Like cattle they branded us, darling, they should only rot in hell. I was a slave to Adolf in Auschwitz. Instead from the gas, we dropped dead from the work." With the plump pad of a fingertip, Luba was suctioning up the crumbs of piecrust that had settled onto the great prow of her bosom. "Yes, darling, it was very terrible, just like they tells you in *Schindler's List*, I wouldn't wish it on a dog, but in the end—I hates to admit this—it all turned out for the best. That's why I gets up every morning and sings 'God Bless America,' even though I'm not a religious person, maybe you even heard me from downstairs. When I came to America I was a nothing, I was a refugee; now, thanks God, I'm a survivor. And mine daughter, Fernie"—she pronounced it "Foinie"—"she even got her career from the whole business, very high class, director from second-generation affairs by the Holocaust Heritage Museum," Luba declared proudly, "maybe you even heard from it, right in the same neighborhood from the Twin Towers, may they rest in peace."

Lola lowered her head as Luba went on, unwinding her spiel. What could she offer? How could she compete with the Holocaust? Lola was Holocaust challenged. The worst thing that had ever happened to her in her entire life was losing her mother when she was a child. She still had not gotten over it, she never would. That was her miserable little Holocaust. Otherwise, there was nothing to distinguish her. Luba would quickly lose interest and then what would Lola do?

"So, darling," Luba burst in suddenly, wiping her mouth and giving Lola a sly look, "the way I figures it, you made up your mind already to finish up on Amsterdam Avenue. In the apartment. Am I right or am I right?"

Silence was translated as confession.

Luba gave out a triumphant laugh. "It also so happens I noticed that you're busy, busy, busy all the time deaccessioning. That's a fancy-shmancy word from the museums, by the way, mine Foinie taught me. It means you're slimming down your collection. You're in a get-rid-get-rid stage—no? Tell me something, darling, is there one single thing still left inside your apartment—a table, maybe, a chair, a bed to sleep on? I says to the super, 'Hector, darling, the minute that lady from downstairs throws out another piece of furniture or some tchotchke, you brings it straight up to me.' So if you ever wants anything back, or maybe you just miss something and you wants to come up and say hello, you know where to find it—one floor up by the elevator, right on tops from you, apartment 4C. All your goods is by me, except for maybe what that *gonif* Hector stole for himself."

Seven more women had to die and require immediate ritual purification and preparation for the grave before Lola could summon up the nerve to get to the point. In the meantime, she and Luba had established a routine. By an unspoken agreement, they refrained from entering one another's apartment; despite Luba's invitation, personal interiors were understood to be off limits, not to be violated. So whenever the phone call came that a fresh lady awaited them in the refrigerator, within half an hour they met in the lobby of their building, and then walked together to the funeral home. Afterward, they always went out for something to eat. "Tradition!" Luba would belt out, linking her arm through Lola's, propelling her to the Utopia, and once in a while, for a change, to one of the other diners, in every single one of which she was recognized and greeted by a chorus. Mostly, it was Luba who talked. She had endless stories, and relished telling and retelling them, fortunately for Lola. But inevitably, Lola was obliged to contribute, do her bit and offer up some morsels from her own stunted life. She had never married—her mother had once said that boys are messy things; somehow that maternal nugget had implanted itself in Lola's brain and taken root—so in the men's department, except for a few boyfriends here and there not worth processing, there was only a vestigial stump. Nevertheless, as she told Luba, she had had many children, all female by gender, from her career as a teacher at a private school for girls. Another mamaism that had stuck with Lola was that education was a very good career for a woman because of the short days and long holidays and vacations—in hindsight, though, she realized that her mother must have been referring not to her, but to real women, with families to care for. She had taught grades one through five over the years, never higher, because even by the fifth grade there would occasionally be some poor girl tormented by precocious physical development who was already bigger than Lola. That brought an appreciative hoot out of Luba, which Lola found exceedingly encouraging. Maybe even she, in her own modest way, could also be entertaining.

Her mother used to tell her how during the endless prayer services in the synagogue of her Galician village, she and her little girlfriends would amuse themselves on the women's balcony by staring in fascination as the wigs of the pious matrons came to life and jitterbugged around on top of their heads—went spastic, like Lola's third graders used to say. Lice, she explained to Luba, who signaled with a nod that of all people, she, Luba

Popkin, a decorated veteran of five death camps, really required no further clarification. And who knows? Maybe her mother's story was the inspiration for Lola's post-retirement second career as a high-end nitpicker.

When Lola hung out her shingle, so to speak, there was a lice plague across the city; for all she knew, maybe there still was. It wasn't just the poor and unwashed, the expendables, who were scratching like dogs; the privileged, pampered children of the rich, such as the ones she taught, were also not exempt. The school nurse inspected heads regularly—just one tiny white nit clinging to a hair, and the kid was sent home, no appeals, no mercy, not even a major contribution to the endowment could alter that reality, no reentry until the all-clear signal was given. Luba probably did not realize just how labor-intensive nitpicking was. You couldn't just charge in there and brutally razor off the entire tangled lice-flecked mops of these little princesses, like in the concentration camps. You couldn't just squat down there, either, like a mama gorilla crouching in her cage, cradling your baby ape in your lap, grooming, grooming, then licking the bug off your finger with your long, wet tongue. You had to go through the head painstakingly, hair by hair, strand by strand, to locate the nits, like a sprinkling of sesame seeds, and also the newborn baby lice, only one millimeter long—Lola wore special goggles with magnifying lenses for this. Naturally, the mothers of these infested children could not be expected to spend such non-quality time going through those colonized heads with a fine-tooth comb, over and over again. It was a job to be delegated; a professional was required. The best person had to be found for this as for all things, money was not an issue. Lola hoped it would not sound like boasting, but she, Lola Blitzer, was the acknowledged best. *New York* magazine had even named her Best Nitpicker. The caption under her picture called her Miss Blitzer the Nitser. For those precious heads, the article made a big point of mentioning, Miss Blitzer applied a special emulsion; the recipe was a family secret handed down from her mother, but Lola had no problem revealing it now to her loyal friend, Luba—one-third olive oil, one-third white vinegar, one-third kerosene—never, God forbid, the official lice shampoos, the only products available on the market, over the counter or prescription, poisons, believe it or not, pesticides and insecticides such as people spread on their lawns, soaking through the scalps of innocent children, seeping directly into their tender, impressionable brains. Furthermore it was noted in this article that, as a veteran teacher, Miss Blitzer made productive use of the time while nitpicking and delousing, conversing with the kids exclusively about educational topics such as great literature, Gitche Gumee and the wigwam of Nokomis, or current events, or space exploration, and playing classical music in the background, Ravel's *Boléro*, over and over again, for relaxing the mind. Luckily or unluckily, this great honor bestowed upon her by the magazine, which included a mahogany plaque that she ordered and paid for but had since thrown out along with everything else—did Luba by any chance have it upstairs in her apartment?—anyway, this newfound celebrity came to Lola around the same time that her eyes, even with the binocular goggles, were giving out, growing too dim and clouded to bear the strain of nitpicking, and the publicity from the article, of course, brought her official attention, so she could no longer safely insist on being paid exclusively in cash. Luba nodded approvingly at this—not for one second in her entire life on American soil had she even considered being paid in anything other than cash—and she confirmed also that many of the tenants in the building had noticed the heavy traffic to and from Lola's apartment during that period; they wondered whether she had a business there, which was strictly prohibited by house rules and regulations, but they were too considerate to report her, they were simply happy for Lola, that finally someone was visiting her.

Lola pushed aside thoughts of allowing the hurt at being universally regarded as pathetic to rise up and engulf her. She went on instead to explain to Luba that obviously the business was limited to afterschool hours and weekends due to the nature of the clientele—unfortunately, it was the same time of day that most people were also home from work; she regretted the disturbance to her neighbors. Almost always the client was delivered by the nanny, but sometimes the mother came along too, usually because she had become infested by her child and required professional treatment herself. There was one mother-daughter case that Lola would never forget. The girl was not even four years old, with very fine flaxen hair. The mother was bringing her child to Lola after having just experienced a life-altering epiphany—she announced this the minute she came through the door. She had stuck her head into the oven along with her daughter's, intending to turn on the gas, to end it all and, mercifully, to take the girl along with her, when she noticed a louse in the child's hair. Immediately she pulled both of their heads out of the oven. There was work to be done, the matter had to be taken care of without delay, she had a purpose on this earth. She called Miss Blitzer. If anyone ever wondered why God created lice, here was the reason.

The seventh woman took away the breath of the entire bereavement committee; even Luba, who believed she had seen everything, was not unshaken. When they entered the room, the overripe steaming up of rot seized them more pungently than ever. She had already been placed inside the coffin, upon the white sheet in which she would be wrapped, now thrown loosely over her. They were ordered to dispense with the purification rites, simply to wash the hands and face and feet. Drawing back the sheet, they were dazed by the raw markings of a freshly stitched autopsy incision, Y-shaped, starting at each shoulder and meeting between the breasts, then plumbing in a straight line down to the pubic zone; another sewn-up incision crossed her forehead, ear to ear. All the organs had been returned to the cavity of the body, they were told, but as they went about their work, a mortuary-science specialist ambled into the room with a lumpy plastic bag and dropped it into the casket with a wet plop. She could not be lifted; her back had already begun to decompose, bacteria lying in ambush had been liberated to start the process, maggots were burrowing. Instead of dressing her, they laid the shrouds on top, then swaddled her as best they could in the white sheet. The women were never told her name or the name of her father, only that she would be buried at the edge of the cemetery, at a distance from other souls. They understood what this meant. She could not have been much more than thirty years old—my mother's age, Lola thought.

At the Utopia afterward, Lola could barely sip her tea. Even Luba's appetite was affected. "No *schlag* for me today, LaToya darling" she said to the waitress. They sat opposite each other in silence, plunged into themselves, broken at last by Luba, who began to tell Lola a story about a butcher, one of the wealthiest merchants in her hometown, who would put his children on the scale every Friday morning and weigh them, and then distribute their weight in meat to the poor for the Sabbath; it was considered a very high act of charity, and inscribed upon his tombstone. "I'm telling you, Lola darling, it's a losing battle. Meat—*fleisch!*—that's what it all boils down to in the end! In the end, the vermins always wins. You thinks you're in control, but I gots news for you, darling."

Luba, at least, was in control until the worms moved in and took over; she had her delegated representative, she had her Fernie to carry out her wishes. Whom did Lola have? Nobody, and nothing. As painful as it was for her to ask for something for herself, as mortifying as it was to even admit that there was something left that she actually still desired on this earth, she tore herself open and turned to Luba.

She needed to be buried next to her mother, in the old Jewish cemetery on Long Island, she said to Luba. She was asking this very great favor of Luba—to take charge when the time came, and make sure this was done. When the time came she would be helpless, at the mercy of others who didn't care two cents about her, that was why she was appealing to Luba, to be her designated driver, to navigate for her, to fight—fight!—on her behalf. She would be forever indebted—unable, of course, to express her gratitude in words when the time came, like the silenced women they prepared for burial, but she would find a way to thank Luba now, in advance, materially and spiritually, with an open hand from the depths of her heart. Instantly, Luba protested that with all the *schlag* in her pipes, she would be the first to go, for sure, whereas Lola's pipes were probably clean as a whistle; Lola was a hermit, a lady monk, like a Hindu in a diaper. No, Lola insisted, Luba was a life force. Luba was indestructible.

The problem was, Lola went on, the plot next to her mother was taken by a complete stranger. There was a narrow strip of earth, a margin at best, between the two plots, her mother's and the stranger's, enough to squeeze in a child maybe, a small child, a ten-year-old maximum—that's what the chief rabbi of the cemetery had told her. Put me in with my mother in the same plot, Lola had cried. The rabbi shook his head. No doubling, no stacking, we've already done mass graves. Even so, he had sold her the sliver of *karka*, as he called it, the mean piece of earth between the two graves, at full price, and she had paid for it joyously, she owned it, she had the receipt—it was her plot. A ten-year-old maximum would be buried there, she had promised him. They had had several meetings to finalize the arrangements but the truth was she didn't trust him—that's why she was turning to Luba to act as her agent and advocate and executor at the appointed hour. During one of her meetings with the rabbi, a boy had walked in with a yarmulke on his head and a knapsack on his back just returned from one of those youth pilgrimages to Poland. From the backpack he drew out a plastic bag filled with pieces of bone he had collected from a garbage dump at one of the death camps—she forgot which camp, maybe it was even Luba's, maybe they were even the bones of Luba's mama. The rabbi agreed to bury the bones in the cemetery—"Yeah, yeah, don't worry, sonny, I'll take care of it," the rabbi said. When the boy left, the rabbi shoved the bag in his desk drawer. Lola believed the bones were still in the rabbi's desk. Lola believed she had already by now reduced herself, through self-denial, through physical discipline and the

The Plot ⋅‣ 71

mortification of her flesh, through fasting and abstinence, to the size of a ten-year-old, maximum. She had been a very good girl; she had given up all sweets. By size, she was now of an age to no longer deserve to be separated from her mother. It was her heart's desire to be buried beside her mother—My mother, Golda. She had earned the privilege, she had already cleansed herself of all impurities and abominations, saving Luba and the rest of the *tahara* bereavement crew a good deal of work and aggravation, setting the record, maybe, for the smallest normal adult corpse they'd ever have to handle, they could process her in five minutes flat and jump right out for a snack. A ten-year-old's coffin customized for the designated space was already set up in her apartment—she fit into it very comfortably now, with lebensraum to spare. Luba would notice it right away when the time came; she couldn't miss it. It was all that remained in the bedroom, with instructions typed out.

She lay on her back inside her coffin, dazed from her mortal combat with sleep, attending to the rush of water from Luba's endless shower above her head. A grinding paralysis had overtaken her. Through the terrifying darkness of the unmoored panic hours, she observed herself struggling to move her limbs, but the dense weight of the air bore down upon her and the sense of impending deluge pressing in would not release her. A scream was lodged in the back of her throat, she labored to push it out, but it was stuck, stuck, she was hoarse from the effort. She must have been able to scream as a child—Sarah Heartburn, that's what her mother used to call her; it seemed the closest of memories. Could it really be so? Could she have ever once indulged in overdramatics, thrown a tantrum, actually treated herself to the redundancy, in her mother's phrase, of a conniption fit? Sarah Bernhardt, a Jewish girl too, also slept in a coffin—it was practice, practice, practice in anticipation of the great farewell performance, illuminating, in the purest sense, the essence of rehearsal. Lola had seen an old sepia postcard—the image of the actress elegantly posed in a pale flowing gown, hair draped around her, long stems of lilies accessorizing her supine form in grand style—a luxurious coffin, befitting a superstar, cushioned with satin. Lola's was the plain pine box of a child, to qualify for admission into the holy graveyard, to fit into her grudging slice of dirt alongside her mother, to pass the rigid standards of the chief rabbi, in strict adherence to Jewish law, it was the flimsiest of barriers against the elements and organisms, the hairy maggots, the coffin flies, the carrion beetles, no nails or metal clamps holding it together to give the illusion of permanence—but for now, for the nights of her own private rehearsals, she padded it with her old quilt, her sagged-out pillow folded under her head, her dear blanket drawn up to her eyes, wide open in the darkness, the coldness of the grave more fearful than death itself.

The master magician Harry Houdini was also laid to rest next to his mother, Mrs. Weiss—that was his wish, his absolute goal; any other place would have been unthinkable—in the old Jewish cemetery in Queens, a station of death on the road to Long Island. Lola would read about Mrs. Weiss's wizard son to her girls sitting cross-legged on the rug in the story corner of their classroom in a circle that emanated from her, she slightly elevated in a child's chair, the book perched upright on her lap to face them, moistening her forefinger and hooking her arm to turn the pages from the far edge, slowly, slowly, like a peep show, in delicious anticipation of what would be revealed. Mrs. Weiss's boy had them under his spell. Heads tilted upward, in concentrated seriousness, they gazed their fill when the picture of his dead body laid out inside his custom-made coffin was fully exposed, the same elaborate bronze model special ordered for his legendary escapes, airtight and impregnable, in which he would have himself sealed and lowered into the black depths. Water engulfed him, but this was not the place where his spirit could bear to come to rest, he had to break free.

She was struggling to break out, but it was as if she were bound up in invisible ropes. Heavy drops of water were falling on her from above with a hypnotic beat, lulling her through the night, streaming, splashing, puddling around her, swelling beneath her, setting her adrift in her little boat. She was hovering above herself, observing herself floating in her child's ark.

From the floor below came crashing noises, doors slamming, heavy rubber boots mounting the stairs. Men in thick leather belts with their gear dangling down, in gray rodent masks, swarmed around her hissing, buzzing. She watched herself as on a screen pinioned in the dead center of their beams. She was the motherless child, Snow White, encircled by laborers with axes and spades, laid out in a glass coffin, frozen, preserved, awaiting the beloved's awakening kiss. Hector, the super, was leaning down toward her, white teeth bared. She could not move her lips. It's not coming from here, she wanted to tell them, it's coming from upstairs, the flood comes from upstairs, run upstairs, she needed to tell them, save her, save her.

Only one man remained now. He threw himself on top of her, crushing her beneath his weight, his mouth open over hers, pumping, pumping, ripping her apart. Panting, he lifted himself to catch his breath, then fell on her again, sucking, sucking. She saw herself under him, helpless and trapped, lashed down as on an altar. She listened as the crate in which she had so carefully packed herself splintered and fractured, cracked like an egg. The shell fell away; she was curled up inside the translucent membrane, powerless to break out, unable to scream. Her mother had instructed her, when cooking or baking, to crack the eggs in a separate bowl, one by one, to examine for blood spots. A blood spot is an impurity, the egg must be thrown out. Blood will soon flow out of your body, her mother had told her, from a place you do not even believe exists; it is a curse, out of your body and into the water. Never leave your baby alone in the water, her mother had warned her. Once upon a time there was a grandmother who called up her daughter on the telephone who left her baby alone in the bathtub to talk to her mother. The baby slipped quietly under the water, sank, and drowned. This is a true story, her mother had said; all stories are true, anything you can imagine can happen.

The men were now tramping and pounding their way across the floor above her, over her head, striking at walls, dragging large objects to scrape out a passageway. The roar of the gushing water, upon which she had tossed through the long night, was suddenly cut off. She detached from her body and flew into the air. Looking up, she saw through the ceiling, through the heavy tub, through the bloated form crumpled inside it, the skin soaked by water, ice blue and shriveled, straight through the masses of flesh to the fist of the untrustworthy heart, now flaccid and cold—the big mama, the survivor who saved only herself, collapsed in the shower. Looking down, she saw herself stretched out, captive and numb. A presence was bending over her as to a baby in a cradle, drained and heaving from sobbing with loneliness all through the night. The face was ravaged, hollow eye sockets spilling slugs like tears. Ma, she wanted to cry out, Ma—but no sound came from her mouth. In vain, she tried to push against invisible barriers to stretch out her arms as the presence withdrew, as it shrank away to a point in the ether and receded out of reach. I am very far away from you, she heard it say over and over again, Very, very far, away, from you—until the words could no longer be heard but hung suspended in the void, over the face of the water.

The House of Love and Prayer

S oon after he turned forty, Rabbi Yidel Glatt died of starvation, self-generated. Not that he had gone on a hunger strike, or had deliberately sought out death in some other way, God forbid. It simply came about naturally as an unintended consequence, so to speak, of his ultra-rigid adherence to the laws of the Torah, many of which he rightly regarded as taking precedence over the grossness of inserting food into your mouth, especially in public, the unseemly wet chewing noises, the Adam's apple bobbing obscenely, the whole mess flushed downward through the body's sewer pipes to its profane end. All of this was a necessary function, of course, and scripturally required to sustain life, but nevertheless simple to expedite quickly and efficiently in most instances by eating the mandated piece of bread the size of an olive (albeit olives can come in a range of sizes), and getting it over with as fast as physically possible. The blessing to be recited before ingesting the olive-sized morsel, on the other hand, and the grace afterward, demanded time and the purest concentration in order to achieve a mystical closeness with God—a closeness, as Rabbi

Yidel taught his small but elite group of followers, that in our day and age, bereft as we are of the holy Temple where once we were able to offer our sacrifices directly, can only be accomplished through uncompromising submission to the laws of the Torah, and through undistracted focus on every syllable of prayer, even the tiniest prepositions and conjunctions, only deceptively inconsequential. From the literal to the spiritual, from the finite to the infinite, this was Rabbi Yidel's mantra. His death set off anguished lamentations among his disciples, who strangely resembled him in their black kaftans and black hats with the extra wide brims from which, like Rabbi Yidel's in his final year, a black veil fell like a shade to prevent their eyes from inadvertently snagging on something forbidden, as they walked wailing behind his earthly remains tightly wound like a scroll in a prayer shawl and carried aloft on a stretcher. They were all without exception strikingly tall and gaunt like their master, two dimensional, as if they were members of the same nearly extinct tribe with a specific body type and a limited life-span. They resembled a procession of medieval monks, passing shadows, ghosts. And, indeed, by the turn of the millennium, every one of them had gone to join Rabbi Yidel in the next world, leaving behind numerous orphans, as the positive injunction to be fruitful and multiply is another animalistic bodily commandment that a man could also dispose of speedily, like eating.

Rabbi Yidel Glatt had appeared on the scene in the late sixties of the last century, full-blown, as if not born of woman. No one knew who he was or where he came from. Later on, when anyone respectfully ventured to inquire, he invariably responded in the words of the sage, Akavyah son of Mahalalel, that he came from a putrid drop. He spoke with an accent of some sort, which grew more or less pronounced depending on the situation, and the needs and level transmitted by his interlocutor, to which he was so sensitively attuned. Most listeners identified this accent as a variation of British or colonial English, though others asserted that it contained the rich inflection and lilt of an educated Middle European, that English was after all his second language. There were even some who claimed to detect in his speech the subtle nuances of a Slav, plucked by the Soviets from the masses at a very early age for intensive training in American English toward a future as a high-powered interpreter or spy, it was conjectured, who, blown away by Israel's stunning triumph in the 1967 Six Day War and the discovery of his identity politics, went off course, and for some unfathomable reason was granted special permission as an early refusenik to emigrate, officially to the Holy Land, though as he often lamented, he had not yet achieved the merit to set foot on that blessed soil.

It was said, however, that as he had made his way westward across the American continent in the belly of the Greyhound toward a predetermined destination that had come to him in a vision, he had stopped off for a few months at a chicken farm in Toms River, New Jersey, owned and operated by Rabbi Sylvan Blech, who in addition to marketing his eggs and fowl on weekdays and attending to his pulpit gig on weekends, significantly increased his income during that turbulent period by training young men of draft age in the laws and techniques of ritual slaughter, after which he ordained them as rabbis by conferring upon them the certificate of smikha, as he was entitled to do, which then allowed his protégés as official clergy or divinity to claim the 4D deferment from military service and thereby avoid early death in the jungles of Vietnam. Those who subscribed to this narrative therefore logically concluded that Rabbi Yidel Glatt was actually an American, and his accent was nothing more than some kind of oratorical enchantment meant to draw in his listeners to the correct path, while the only definitive message others took from tales of his chicken farm sojourn in his wanderings through the wilderness of America was that, if true, it merely served to explain his extreme veganism, and perhaps also, in retrospect, to provide some insights into many of his other food issues, which ultimately brought about his death.

It should be noted, though, that the Russia scenario acquired a fresh burst of credibility when further accounts of Rabbi Yidel's epic crossing of the face of the American continent placed him for a period of time in Boulder, Colorado, where, according to reliable sources, he underwent the ritual of circumcision. With regard to these reports, the American-origins camp, while of course insisting on respecting Rabbi Yidel's privacy, asserted that as the son of militantly secular pseudo-sophisticated Jewish intellectuals who disdained what they regarded to be a primitive and barbaric rite and believed they knew better than generations of their forebears, either he had not been circumcised at all, or, due to the health benefits circumcision is alleged to possess, the procedure was performed on him by a medical provider soon after birth as nothing more than routine minor surgery, therefore making it necessary for Rabbi Yidel to reenact it as a brit milah by extracting the requisite drop of blood from the tip of his dedicated organ, collecting it on a white napkin of some sort, and displaying it to three witnesses. The Russia camp, for its part, hammered in the point that Jews from the rabidly anti-religion Soviet State were almost universally never circumcised, and though Rabbi Yidel Glatt might have been one of the earliest to be let out from that dark side, this fact was confirmed again and again over the next decades, as Russian Jews poured into the luminous free world lugging their musical instruments, including pianos. Thanks to the benevolent outreach of so many good and charitable organizations, thousands upon thousands of circumcisions were performed on these newcomers, who voluntarily came forward to offer themselves up on the altar of their recovered faith, even men with organs that had seen so much action in that sexually permissive, secular state, so much wear and tear over their average life expectancy span of fifty-nine years. The model, after all, was Father Abraham, the first man to enter the covenant, ninety-nine years old at the time of his brit, according to the Hebrew Bible.

Rabbi Yidel, for his part, was not yet twenty-five, a thumb-sucker by comparison, but still he was fully entrenched in the tradition of Father Abraham, and like Father Abraham, he is said to have circumcised himself. There were only two other men present in the room, the mohel wielding the knife and a witness, a quorum of ten circumcised males was not required for such late initiation into the covenant, so the report of what transpired within those four walls must have been leaked by one of those two, certainly not by Rabbi Yidel, who was meticulous in his personal reserve and discretion. And who could blame them? It must have been a gevaldig moment, tremendous, the need to tell somebody must have been intense. Suddenly, Rabbi Yidel lurched out of the chair of Elijah, properly zealous to perform the mitzvah, the sooner the better, as our sages encourage us. He grabbed the knife from the mohel's hand and, without the benefit of any anesthetic other than the high of his personal fervor, made the cut himself before either of the two men realized what was happening or could do anything to intervene. Then he folded himself over at the waist like a pita, so flexible and supple was he thanks to the absence on his long, lean frame of even an ounce of extra flesh, placed his own mouth on the sacred crown of his covenant, and personally performed upon himself the mezizah, sucking up the blood. Afterward, he stretched out his hand, and the mohel, weeping loudly along with the witness at this overwhelming display of extraordinary righteous ardor, as if under a spell, docilely handed him the instruments to sew the sutures necessary on a mature organ. Rabbi Yidel did an excellent job, according to insider reports, it came out looking like a proper yarmulke with perfect stitching on the rim. When it was all done, he didn't coddle himself for a minute, but shot up again out of Elijah's chair, seized the hands of the mohel and the witness, and all three men danced around in a circle singing ecstatically the words intoned at the circumcision of an eight-day-old boy, *May this little one become big, ya-ba-bum.* It is also reported that before parting, they drank a celebratory glass of schnapps and ate a piece of matjes herring off a toothpick topped with a red cellophane frill, but this detail is very hard to believe as Rabbi Yidel was by then already one hundred percent vegan.

Without sparing himself a minute, Rabbi Yidel accepted a ride with the mohel from Boulder to the Greyhound terminal in Denver, where he boarded the bus to San Francisco, which was just about to pull out, but instead, thanks to personal divine intervention, paused, dipped courteously, opened its doors, and welcomed him in. After two days in the belly of the dog on harrowing grinding roads, like the prophet Jonah tossed about in the belly of the great fish, he arrived limping in San Francisco and made his way to the legendary synagogue and hostel, the House of Love and Prayer, located in the orbit of the hippie Haight-Ashbury mecca, in order to carry out his mission of speaking his prophecy to its inmates that they must change their ways at once lest the whole edifice come tumbling down on their heads. There, still tender and aching but never complaining, the hand of God displayed itself to him once again by causing the door of the House of Love and Prayer to be opened by a complete stranger, Terry Birnbaum, known as Tahara. She had been waiting for him as he had been journeying toward her the whole time—she had prepared for his arrival by purifying herself in the ritual bath as her name implied, while, for his part, the mark he had made upon his own body was also meant for her. When they saw each other they both accepted this truth instantly. They were manifestly each other's destiny, there was no other explanation and no escape, it was God's will.

She was eighteen years old, from a bagels-and-lox family on the Upper West Side of Manhattan, had dropped out of NYU after only one month spent mostly sleeping all day and sitting all night stoned at the feet of Reb Lionel Ziprin, kabbalist and mystic, breathing in his poetry and songs in his mother's Lower

East Side apartment smelling of old age, where he presided. On her last night in Reb Lionel's forcefield, he zoomed in on her perched there swaying on the carpet sucking on a joint and said, as if in a prophetic trance, "Go west, young lady, there you will find what you are seeking."

That, at least, was how she told the story to her eleven children and countless grandchildren years later. The next day she bundled some stuff in a madras cloth, tied it into a knot, slung it over her shoulder, and set out hitchhiking across the land. The many adventures she encountered as she made her way across the wild frontier toward the setting sun was something she would never detail to her children, it was enough for her to warn them that her own heart would crack in pieces if any of them tried a stunt like that and followed in her footsteps; she had been a tiny girl in those days, not even five feet tall and no more than ninety pounds, with long black hair parted in the middle flowing straight down her back and so fresh and pretty, if she must say so herself, no shoes on her feet and no money in her pocket, evil people took advantage, outlaws and bandits and desperados and other assorted bad guys, that was as much as she was willing to share. By the time she reached the House of Love and Prayer in San Francisco and the door was opened to her by its center of gravity, its guru, Rabbi Shlomo Carlebach himself, troubadour, minstrel, and pied piper, she was seriously damaged, polluted, filthy. "Oy, do you need a fixing," Reb Shlomo said, after taking one look at her. He asked her name. "You no longer will be called Terry," he intoned in his Teutonic singsong. "From this day forward, your name will be Tahara"—and he sent her off with one of the women to be ritually purified in the mikvah.

The next months she passed awaiting the arrival of Rabbi Yidel Glatt, though of course she understood this only retrospectively. She spent her days studying the healing arts, holistic medicine, acupuncture, wellness, massage, macrobiotic diets, organic farming, the power of crystals and stones and beads, mushrooms and cannabis, and so on, and at night she gathered with all the other lost souls at Reb Shlomo's feet, getting higher and higher on his songs and streaming on his stories so that it was nothing less than an honor in those pre-dawn hours when the heart is clamped with dread to be the girl summoned to his chamber for warmth and further instruction. When she opened the door to Rabbi Yidel that day, he so tall and she so small, it was palpably and undeniably clear that she was his missing rib, she had been created to complete him. At last she understood the true meaning of the oracle pronounced by the holy fool, Reb Lionel, she knew why she had to come so far through such treacherous and alien territory, everything was clarified. A week after they met at its door, Tahara and Rabbi Yidel Glatt were married at the House of Love and Prayer in a wedding so fabulous it spilled out into the streets and lasted for three days and three nights of rejoicing, it was the mythic rave party that wouldn't stop climaxing.

Those paying attention, however, could not help but notice that although the marriage ceremony itself took place under the stars in front of the House of Love and Prayer, Reb Shlomo's turf, Reb Shlomo himself was not the one asked to officiate, nor was he included among the distinguished rabbinical personages called up to stand under the wedding canopy and offer one of the seven blessings, or, for that matter, was he given any honor at all. All of these honors were bestowed on rabbinical figures with credentials for the strictest observance and piety imported by Rabbi Yidel Glatt to San Francisco from Los Angeles, where contrary to popular preconceptions, such people truly could be found, they exist, they are not actors. Reb Shlomo and his inner circle of sinners were unqualified to perform his wedding, this was Rabbi Yidel's absolute conviction, by no stretch did they live up to his standards. For the sake of drawing in all those turned-off spoiled Jewish kids, and of capturing the souls of the whole congregation of Jewish losers, they took license to indulge all their evil inclinations, they were sinners in all their appetites, above the waist and below. Their participation in his marriage, other than as ordinary guests, would render it one hundred percent pasul, unkosher, invalid, according to Rabbi Yidel Glatt.

Within an hour after he had sealed his betrothal with Tahara, following which they did not see each other again until their wedding itself, Rabbi Yidel Glatt stationed himself immediately inside the House of Love and Prayer, his back to the door, and he boomed out, "Don't give me your New Ageism, your Interfaith Dialogue, your Jewish Renewal, your tikkun olam, your Holocaust idolatry, your self-indulgent practice, your lax observance, your counterculture, your Hin-Jew, your Jew-Bude, your two-state solution, your final solution, or whatever other solution your sick minds can cook up. If you don't change your ways immediately, if not sooner, your whole House will come crashing down, the ravenous earth of this pagan city named for a gentile so-called saint will open up its ugly maw and swallow you up, like Korakh and his gang of sinners."

After that he shut down, entering into a fast of silence as well as a fast of eating for the entire week until his wedding day, parking himself those full seven days and nights like a Standing Baba on his spot right inside the House of Love and Prayer, a tall shockingly slender tree blackened by the fire of faith, the top of his black hat almost grazing the ceiling, his arms raised to the heavens as if in prayer like the arms of Moses our Teacher overlooking the plain of the wilderness below as the Jews battled the Amalekites. For seven days Rabbi Yidel Glatt stood there, transforming himself into an obstacle, an impediment, anyone who wanted to enter or leave had to factor him in, to take him into account, to consider him and what he stood for literally and figuratively in order to get around him and get past him. He broke his fast of what went into his mouth under the wedding canopy with a sip of the blessed wine, and of what came out of his mouth with the words he pronounced to Tahara without looking at her, "Behold you are consecrated to me, and so forth." On the seventh day after their wedding, her shaved head bound up in a turban woven from azure Indian silk shot through with gold thread, Tahara set out from the House of Love and Prayer, this time under the protection of the looming scythe-like figure of her husband, Rabbi Yidel Glatt, hitchhiking back eastward together across the fruited plain. By the time they reached Brooklyn and settled in their tiny apartment with a fire escape over a ritual bath, prophetically called Mikvah Tahara, on Forty-Third Street in the ultra-religious Borough Park neighborhood, she was already noticeably pregnant with her first.

As the babies came, one after the other like clockwork, Rabbi Yidel Glatt, who earned a small income teaching in the apartment, was forced to move his classes out to the fire escape when the weather cooperated. There he could talk Torah in peace and quiet among the pots in which his wife Tahara grew her herbs and God alone knew what else, which, according to their landlady, Mrs. Bella Cohen, was also against city codes—to clutter the fire escape with junk—they were in violation on at least two counts, she would have to talk to them, give them a piece of her mind. Mrs. Cohen was completely unmoved by the fact that Rabbi Yidel Glatt refused to charge for his teachings in accordance with the injunction of the sages against using the Torah as an axe to chop with, meaning, bottom line, as he interpreted it, that it was forbidden to make money from Torah. As far as Mrs. Cohen was concerned, business was business; whatever this meshuggeneh guru chose to do was his own private business, he personally did not need to eat at all it seemed, even if his children starved. Without a doubt his Hasidim left money for him somewhere on the fire escape when he held his classes up there, Mrs. Cohen figured, probably under the pots. The little wife would go out afterward to search, it was her job to hunt for the treasure, that way her holy husband's hands stayed spotlessly clean, untainted, Glatt kosher, ha ha, the money would just drop down like manna, like a miracle from heaven, the sin would not fall upon his head. Naturally his Hasidim gave him money, it goes without saying, Mrs. Cohen maintained, he was their rebbe, their master, that's how it was done the world over, that's how rebbes got their Cadillac limos and their first class plane tickets to Israel and their top-of-the-line sable Davey Crockett hats.

In cold weather, or in the pouring rain or snow, Rabbi Yidel delivered his teaching in the back room of Butch Pincus's shop, known as TattJoos, on the fringe of the neighborhood. He had run into Butch in the lot on Eighteenth Avenue where he and his Hasidim would gather each month to bless the new moon, the closest a person could come to the Divine presence, as Rabbi Yidel taught. Butch was a regular in the darkness of that lot, though it was known to be not such a safe place, filled with hungering souls prowling among the garbage and the rats, the used syringes and the used rubbers. One night, as Rabbi Yidel and his boys came out to greet the new moon, to sing directly into the ear of God under the open sky, pouring their hearts out like water in gratitude to Him for the light of this monthly renewal, Butch joined them in prayer, chanting flawlessly word for word from memory. It was clear that here among them was an authentic insider who had lapsed, strayed—the former BenZion Pincus, a descendant of certified rabbinical royalty no less, Rabbi Yidel soon discovered, who, as was well known in this Brooklyn ghetto, had gone seriously beyond the pale of settlement, straight into hell's kitchen, bringing shame and grief to his illustrious family—in the excremental language of the written law, trafficking in the ka'ka business, this Pincus, tattoos, which as Rabbi Yidel knew, the Torah forbids one hundred percent.

Butch invited them into his parlor where he proceeded to spin his case for the legitimacy of tattooing despite the seemingly stringent prohibition against such forms of so-called self-mutilation as expounded in the book of Leviticus. "What is circumcising the flesh of your foreskin if not the number one tattoo in the history of mankind?" Butch insisted. "What does it mean to set a seal upon a heart? To place totafot between your eyes? Don't give me that bullshit about the image of God, the sanctity of the body," Butch declaimed. "Where was God with His sanctity when the murderers tattooed us in the death camps? Now by freely choosing to tattoo ourselves we turn anguish to joy, mourning to holiday, we adorn ourselves in the spirit of renewal, we re-sanctify our bodies, as we re-sanctify and renew our moon each month." He, Butch Pincus, specialized in Jewish tattoos, he could show them some designs, they could choose if they were so inclined, or they could go creative and custom design their own, or they could just stick with the basic model already cut into their flesh, the mark of their covenant hanging there plain and forlorn between their legs, if that was their preference, no pressure. Meanwhile, they were welcome to use the backroom of his tattoo parlor for their meetings when the weather was inclement, free of charge except for regular cleanings of the premises, maybe by one of their wives.

For this cleaning job, Tahara received no direct payment, since it was effectively a swap, but here too, in Pincus's shop, among the needles and inks and the sinister devices, she found in hidden places the bills that Rabbi Yidel's followers left for their master so as not to sully him by depositing payment directly into his hands. Her other cleaning job, one that Mrs. Cohen had offered her in exchange for a reduction in the rent, was at the mikvah, to keep the place immaculate, wash it down every day—a sanitary, hygienic bathhouse was priority number one, absolutely nonnegotiable. For an added discount, Mrs. Cohen also called upon Tahara regularly to supervise the immersions of some of the ladies, in particular those who asked for her by name, more and more customers as time passed, she was still so tiny, though maybe not so svelte like she used to be due to all those babies, she was no threat at all, such a cute little roly-poly doll—the place, after all, was called Mikvah Tahara, it was only right, she was a terrific draw, very good for business and, bottom line, it was also a very good deal for that woman of valor, the Rebbetzin Tahara Glatt, whose rent bill in the end came down to bubkes, Mrs. Cohen noted.

So it was not at all surprising that when Rabbi Yidel Glatt entered the mikvah for the last time on that warm spring night, he found his wife on duty. In truth, she was working there almost full time by then, while their eldest, Sora Malka, fifteen years old already, looked after all the other children upstairs in the apartment. Though Rabbi Yidel knew very well that the nights were reserved for immersion by wives under the cover of darkness for the sake of privacy with regard to their monthly cycles and conjugal rhythms, the need to purge himself had suddenly gripped him overwhelmingly and would not pass. His black rubber glove, as if concealing a prosthesis, glistened under the newly blessed moon as he stretched out his hand to open the door with his personal key, his tense shallow breaths fluttered the veil rippling down from the halo of his black hat.

He encountered her instantly, in the waiting room, straightening out a pile of glossy magazines devoted to the Jewish woman and the Jewish home. She gazed at him, this was her husband, so tall and wasted, like a long dried-out reed that could snap at the slightest breath, and without uttering the words, her eyes spoke—What are you doing here? You know it's ladies' night. He thought maybe business was slow, he said, maybe there was a chance he could have a dunk. She had made a big pot of soup with kasha, strictly vegan naturally, Go upstairs and eat something, she said. He wasn't hungry, he replied, he didn't want to think about food, food interfered with his spiritual quest, it clogged his passageways, it came between him and God. Why was she bothering him with food at such a time?

Instead of answering, she rummaged in the pile of magazines, pulled one out, and held it up straight in front of his face, almost grazing his nose, she pushed it so aggressively close he could barely make out the words, the letters merged into a mushroom cloud. *Anorexia Nervosa*, he read finally the bold headline on its cover, *An Epidemic in Our Community*, and the background picture was of religious Jewish women of all ages, their faces blotted out for reasons of modesty, the outlines of their blurred bodies nevertheless visible even under their shapeless wardrobes, emaciated like classic concentration camp inmates, like scarecrows. It has nothing to do with God, she was telling him, bent on administering a therapeutic dose of tough love, so stop blaming God already. It's an eating disorder, what you have, a body image thing, she said—it's not just women's troubles, she said, men get it too, like breast cancer.

He bowed his head and nodded. It was true, he was privileged to be suffering from women's troubles, he granted her that, though he doubted she could penetrate the full depths of his holy affliction. In the most mystical of texts forbidden to almost all eyes, it was revealed that the messiah would be born not from a woman but from the bowels of a man, which despite the presence of waste matter was infinitely preferable to the blood-soaked womb and the polluted canal, even of a virgin. He was pregnant with the messiah. He longed to share this news with Tahara, but held back. Still, it remained his responsibility to limit the intake of food even more strictly, in order to keep his entrails as clean as possible, out of respect for the gestating deliverer. All this was information she was not yet spiritually ready to receive, he recognized. Instead, he ventured only to ask her to do him a kindness now, to enlarge the rear portion of his black trousers by sewing in a sac or a pouch of some sort, for the sake of comfort and modesty was what he told her, but in truth to catch the messiah, should he unexpectedly slip out, lest the holy redeemer fall to the ground and injure himself, God forbid, when he comes blinking into this world in a good hour.

It was as if his words entered the atmosphere and vaporized, they passed her by categorically, she blocked them so completely. "Why do you have that shmatteh flapping from your hat, covering up your whole face?" she only went on demanding. "And what's this business now with the glove? Is this normal?" Stricken with pity for her limitations, Rabbi Yidel Glatt answered with head bowed, his voice barely audible, reminding her that Moses our Teacher also wore a veil, after sitting with God on the mountaintop for forty days and forty nights, eating no bread and drinking no water, God's beams were imprinted on his face, the light was too much for ordinary mortals to bear.

He left the mikvah and climbed the stairs up to their apartment to complete his dying, which took about a week. One by one, all of his systems and organs shut down from the consequences of starvation, until finally his heart gave out. Out of pity for the mother who bore him but whom she had never known,

Tahara tended to him faithfully day and night throughout his dying—palliative care, home hospice she called it approvingly. He sat as if propped up in a wooden straight-backed chair, fully dressed like a Russian who having completed the preparations for a long journey, sits down and pauses to reflect before setting out, in his black kaftan and rope belt, his hat with the black veil firmly on his head and the black glove still sheathing his left hand. He refused to allow Tahara to remove any of his clothing, wrapping his withered arms around the jutting ribs of his hollow chest and shrieking horrifyingly whenever she ventured to loosen even a button. His followers, also in their long black kaftans and black hats with their veils attached, kept vigil in the hallway outside the apartment, on the stairs, and throughout the building including the mikvah, to the annoyance and frustration of Mrs. Bella Cohen—but unfortunately, there was nothing she could do about it, she was stuck. The man, after all, was dying.

The final agony lasted over two days of fierce suffering with no relief, until Rabbi Yidel Glatt's soul visibly left his body through his mouth and out the open window in a long translucent rope, like intestines unraveling. It was only when the agony began to consume him that Tahara, with the help of her daughter, Sora Malka, was able to lift him up out of his chair, he was so shrunken, practically weightless, as if he had been completely emptied out, and lay him on his bed. Only then was Tahara able to take off his outer garments for the sake of easing his passage to the next world.

As he gasped for breath nonstop over the two days of the death rattle, hyperventilating desperately in shrill grating whistles and terrible dry cries scraped up from the depths of his cavernous being that shook the walls of their building and spilled out into the streets, Tahara sat at his side and kept watch. Now that his outer garments had been removed and he lay there like the excavated remains of a rare prehistoric creature, she could see at last how he had achieved the momentous permanent binding to the Divine for which he had so fervently longed and so obsessively striven all the years she had known him. Spiraling up his left arm and wrapped around his head were tattooed the black straps of a full set of phylacteries, the two black tefillin boxes with their parchment verses also visible gashed into his flesh, one on his inner arm pointing toward his heart, the other on top his head, *totafot* tattooed between his eyes. He had cut God into his own flesh, incised God as a permanent sign upon his own body, slashed God's words into his heart and brain in uttermost subjection to the commandment. This was the reality to which Tahara now surrendered herself and accepted, but there were those outside their sphere who could never comprehend, she knew, it would look to them like transgression not longing, blasphemy not devotion, madness not passion. She made a mental note to herself that after it was all over, his followers, surely marked as he was by Pincus the tattoo artist, must be the ones designated to carry out the ritual known of all things as the *tahara*—they alone must be the ones to privately perform the purification of the body for burial, she would insist on that. Any other member of the community, the regulars of the holy burial society, simply wouldn't get it, they would see what Rabbi Yidel had done to himself, misinterpret it as a form of idolatry, maybe even seek to block his interment in the cemetery, it would be an intolerable end to his story that she could never sit by and allow.

Thirty days after his passing, it began to be heard all around that Rabbi Yidel Glatt was, after all, not even Jewish. At first it seemed like nothing more than a spiteful rumor, but it didn't fade away like an ordinary rumor. To the contrary, it grew and deepened and spread like a malignant plague—a Jew-impersonator in our midst of the most extreme and grotesque type, a caricature, a self-created stereotype, the worst kind of anti-Semite—so that the day soon arrived when the head of the board of the cemetery in which Rabbi Yidel Glatt was buried came to Tahara and requested that the body be removed with a full refund, not because of the tattoos, no, the rejection by a Jewish cemetery of a tattooed Jew was just an urban myth, like crocodiles swimming among the turds in the sewers of New York City. It is simply because in accordance with our bylaws, the chairman of the board advised Tahara, non-Jews are forbidden an eternal resting place within the walls of our cemetery.

In the darkness of a moonless night, overseen by the widow, Rabbi Yidel Glatt's followers went in and disinterred him. Those who glimpsed his remains asserted that he did not in death appear in any way different from how he had looked in life; it was the sign of a true holy man, they said. He was reburied elsewhere, to this day no one knows the exact spot, lest people come to worship at his gravesite, like Moses our Teacher who also wore a veil to shield onlookers from his radiance. In time, whether true or not, without benefit of any further proof, it became universally accepted as common knowledge—Rabbi Yidel Glatt was a gentile. For those for whom he had officiated as rabbi in such matters as conversion, marriage, divorce, the consequences were shattering, catastrophic, rendering all of his pastoral interventions invalid, all subsequent marriages and remarriages null and void, and all of the children from those marriages bastards and mongrels born in sin and banned from admittance to the assembly of the Lord even to the tenth generation.

The Page Turner

For once they all agreed, it would be the concert of the season, the return of the prodigy son. The Jerusalem music scene was in heat—survivors, empty-seat fillers, remnants planted on their subscriptions, but from the neck up, in brainpans that went on ticking, still the strictest standards, the highest expectations. My mother, Sonia Frankel the piano teacher, she too among them, and also my father Hirsch the tailor, they also caught the fever. They all remembered him from his one and only appearance, not just in Jerusalem but in all of Israel, thirty, maybe forty, years ago, a teenager with braces on his teeth and pimples on his face and those bangs, now static gray still absurdly fringing his brow, hiding recession: Rudi Plaszcynski, a big meaty kid over six feet tall, each hand like a raw five pound slab of chuck with the thumb on the scale, but on the keyboard, the pure, light touch of an angel and a rigor that might even have redeemed the sins of the fathers, every note absorbed internally and delivered with eyes squeezed shut, flawlessly from memory—by heart, only by heart!

Perfection—anything less he despised as weakness, utter

intolerance for the mediocre, that was Plaszcynski, for whatever he regarded as second rate, nothing but contempt. So it was a double shock to the faithful when his handlers let it be known that not only was he coming back like the ghost of a boy genius after so many decades, but also that he was demanding a page turner, "The best your fake little country can offer." It was one thing to refuse to play for Jews all those years, this was a reality the fans could absorb thanks to their diaspora mindset, the chronic mentality of transients, aliens, guests in someone else's house; Jews were meant to practice hard and play on demand for others, to please, like nowadays the Chinese, they were not put on this planet to be entertained, it was beneath a proud artist of Plaszcynski's stature to lower himself by performing for them, which maybe explained, even justified, his long absence—but a page turner? What happened to his principles, his standards, his dignity, his *heart*? "Plaszcynski, Shmasz-cynski, I think he must be drying up," my father concluded. "So now he'll hold a beauty contest to pick the next Queen Esther to turn his pages—but first he'll have to try her out for a night." He said this to me, my own bitter father, he didn't hold back, even though he knew very well that in a tiny country like Israel, not to mention a provincial village like Jerusalem, with zero degrees of separation, the likelihood was that the page turner that Plaszcynski would crown would be me.

It was something I did on a moonlighting basis, after my day job filling book orders deep in the stacks of the National Library—freelance page turning. This was all that was left of my mother's big dreams for my concert artist career, my mother, my first and most unforgiving piano teacher, leaning over my practice, poisoned by visions of me gliding across the stage in flowing blacks, I was her personal revenge against Hitler, she would say, Nekama, she would call me, twisting my name, Nekhama, vengeance, not consolation. Always she balanced on the lip of disappointment, my damaged mother, and I sprouted into a major disappointment, instead of public acclaim I sought out invisibility, which is the definition of page turning at its most exquisite. Still, despite my vanishing act, or perhaps due to its allure of exclusivity, I had somehow acquired the reputation as the Holy Land's page turner of choice for all the top visiting artists who came to town, with impresarios asking for me by name, Plaszcynski included, but he insisted that two more options also be delivered for the final round so he could have his choice among the chosen people, women only, he considered anything else unnatural, perverted, all three of us runners-up skinny almost to transparency, two-dimensional like shadows, ideal in the page-turning business, Polish-speaking Jewish women with dark circles under our eyes and faces like photos in expired passports found in a pile.

We were herded in front of him in his suite at the Mishkenot Sha'ananim cultural center for artists and scholars and other similar specimens, which was equipped with a Steinway grand, dressed as preordered in our concert blacks, no jewelry, no bracelets or bangles or rings, of course, but also no earrings that could jangle, no necklaces that could swing and swat while turning a page, maybe even blinding a virtuoso. He, for his part, met us in mismatched pajamas, orange polka-dotted bottoms, and green-striped top, buttoned lopsided exposing patches of raw skin and tight coils of hair, a red stocking hat with a fat pompom, and fuzzy slippers. The next hour or so was passed with him inhaling every part of us; any hint of a

smell would have been intolerable, from makeup and per-
fumes and toiletries to food and body odors, and so on to the
unmentionable. Addressing us exclusively in Polish, assessing
our comprehension level in the process, he ordered us to open
our mouths, raise our arms, he was like a master shopping for
a slave, like a dog going straight for our privates and sniffing.
"There's such a thing as a Jewish smell, nothing personal, but
you can't deny it," he allowed himself to remark. He brought
his ear up to our faces to listen for breathing noises, an instant
disqualifier. He lined us up for height, examined our fingernails
for jagged ridges, measured the length of our arms extended for
reach, checked our vision for distance. The only thing he didn't
bother with was examining us for music-reading skills, in this
way signaling, now that I look back, that he really didn't need
us, for us he had something else in mind. Then he sat down at
the piano, flipped open some music to a random place, and
started playing to sample our page-turning techniques—how
alertly we moved, how silently and unobtrusively, how we
leaned over without drawing attention to ourselves and neatly
drew back one page and one page only from the top right-hand
corner with two fingers of our left hand, without spit lubricant
or ruffling the airwaves, while with the right hand we held in
place any loose garments or body protrusions lest they brush
against his person, disgust and distract him, an operation at
which one of my colleagues fumbled, and with a push of the
flattened heel of his great paw on her hollowed-out chest was
eliminated.

"Three points for anyone who recognizes this," he rang out
without lifting his foot from the pedal for a minute.

"Aeolian Harp—Chopin, Opus 25, Étude no.1 in A-flat

Major," I said in a voice that he must at least not have found too painful, though the page he had opened to had something else on it entirely, and though I had never heard this piece played so loud or so slow, like a funeral march, it was almost unrecognizable.

"The program will be all Chopin études, technically among the most challenging in the literature," he continued—"to honor the heroic Polish people, the saviors of you Jews for centuries, when nobody else would take you in—why doesn't anyone ever remember to say thank you?" He was notorious for putting off announcing the program until the last minute, as close as possible to concert time, a big headache for the publicity team, it was always entirely dependent on his mood, the creative spirit which required full deference, he waited for that spirit to seize him and reveal what would flow out of him through his fingers on that night. This scoop pointedly directed at me clearly was a privileged preview. I understood that I had been chosen. He handed me the dry cleaner's receipt for his tuxedo, and ordered me to pick it up and have it ready for him with all accessories laid out in the green room of the concert hall one hour on the dot before curtain time.

Yet there he was out on the stage in the hour before the recital's scheduled start still in his polka-dotted and striped pajamas and elf's cap and cozy slippers, propped at the piano, not sitting but prancing up and down alongside the keyboard, his right leg stretched precariously out and down to pin the foot to the pedal, perfecting his new variation of the étude. Audience members were filing in, finding their seats, settling down, making themselves comfortable, going through their routines, unwrapping and distributing lozenges, exchanging news about the children and grandchildren with old friends and acquaintances, many from the same shtetls and death camps, as they tended to reserve their seats in blocs based on where they came from in the old country, in the same way that they reserved their plots in cemeteries.

Some kind of clown sideshow was happening on stage, they figured, a bonus attraction, a creative twist on the business of pre-recital piano tuning, but never mind, Israel was filled with all kinds of meshuggenehs, so why not crazy piano-tuners also? Most didn't even realize that it was the artist himself skipping around up there in that bizarre getup, but my father, from his seat alongside my mother front row center, where I always planted them thanks to my perks and protectzia in the music scene, called out under his breath in Polish, "Plaszcynski, Plaszcynski, enough already with the monkey business!"—and he jutted his jaw emphatically in the direction of the open doorway stage left to focus the star's attention on where I had stationed myself, condemned to hold up his black tails on a hanger, the sleeves stuffed with tissue paper extended like a crucifix, wordlessly signaling to him that it was time already, for God's sake, come and get dressed. In answer, Plaszcynski puffed out his cheeks for added visual effect, blowing up and down the keyboard, gentle winds like the god Aeolus of the étude, and then, according to my mother's account afterward, he let out fiercer winds, yes, it was unmistakable to the nose hairs, he was shamelessly passing wind nonstop like a comment on the audience as he shuffled sideways off the stage toward where I had positioned myself, doffing his absurd cap in grand sweeping gestures again and again as he made his way bowing repeatedly into the wings to the sound of scattered applause from some members of the crowd whom none of us recognized, round red faces and bad dental work, most likely cleaning or security staff from the Polish consulate who had gotten free tickets.

He took his time getting dressed, totally unmindful of the rhythmic clapping from the audience growing more and more insistent, reaching a crescendo a full twenty minutes past the scheduled starting hour of the concert. When finally he strode unrepentantly out ten minutes later, there was some hopeful applause expressing a good-hearted resolve to forgive and start fresh. I placed the music on the stand and took my seat angled slightly forward to his left, alert beside his bench, somewhat set back but still blocked by his bulk, with my hands resting ready on my knees. Without making any adjustments for height and distance, he plunked his bottom on the padded quilted bench, which gave out an impolite poof, parked his right foot on the pedal from which he never lifted it for almost the entire evening, and plunged at once into the first étude of Opus 10, "Waterfall," at a dirge-like tempo stridently fortissimo, stretching out what usually ran for two and a half minutes to more than five. He kept this up for the second étude into the third, running them together without a break. Each time I got up to turn a page, it was as if I were pushing slow motion through a gelatinous soup, but he never even glanced at the music. I had no idea what he wanted me for; it crossed my mind that I might have been set up as his personal straight man.

By the time he reached No. 4, known as "Torrent," there was an epidemic of coughing followed by a buzzing in the crowd as citizens began to absorb what might be their fate through all twelve études of Opus 10, and maybe also onward into all twelve of Opus 25, scrolling out nonstop with no promise of relief, and possibly, God forbid, even the three extra loose études not part of an official opus thrown in as an encore, whether we clamored for one or not. About a minute into No. 4, without letting up on the banging, he whipped his head around to face the audience and shouted over the torrent in English, in a thick Polish accent, "Stup tawkink!" From one of the back rows, some wise guy feeling entitled and secure in his own land under the protection of the crack Israel Defense Forces, yelled back in Polish, "You start playing, we stop talking!" "Shot op!" Plaszcynski screamed back, never for a minute resting from the pounding, as this antagonist who had dared to defy him rose from his seat and swaggered to an exit, followed by a band of others from around the hall, seasoned partisans heading to the woods.

Ignoring them as beneath his regard, Plaszcynski crashed into No. 5, "Black Keys," the whole time his head turned to the right glaring menacingly at what was left of the audience, daring them to misbehave and risk provoking him. A respectable crowd still remained in the hall, including my parents, so prominently positioned, sticking it out from loyalty to me, to protect me, to rescue me from this hostile Slav if necessary, nothing Plaszcynski could do would make them budge. Every ember snatched from the fire still holding out in that audience was on best behavior like in school, sitting nicely for fear of serious consequences, dreading being singled out by this certified cultural demigod for public humiliation as an ignoramus and a philistine, reluctant to endure full-body exposure by getting up and shuffling out with their walkers and sticks and other assorted paraphernalia, loathe to throw out the good money of a ticket, even with the senior citizen or season discount. It was like what my father would always say about those who didn't pick themselves up in time and get out while they still could during those years: Because they didn't know what to do with their furniture, they died for their stuff.

Unmoved by the pathetic protest of the deserters, Plaszcynski legattoed directly into No. 6, "Lament," jamming down on the pedal with even greater force as if to accentuate the relevance of sorrow in this benighted place, exalted music wasted on such a crass mob, squeezing every last shred of vibration from the notes and prolonging them even more, stretching out the étude's less than three minutes to more than seven, which included a condescending glance cast in the direction from which a cell phone went off with the opening bars of the Israeli national anthem, "Hatikvah," and then, shamed, was immediately neutralized. When he ended that étude at last, he got up for the one and only time during this recital, lumbered to the edge of the stage, and said in English, "Smetana dat Czech drunkard, his little tune in minor key maybe okay for sentimentalist Zionist, but for true artist, he is *gowno* next to Polish genius Chopin. You are in concert hall, I must to remind you, ladies and gentlemen, not Israel Knesset." He turned decisively, sat down again without ceremony and continued to dirge out his thunderous, protracted renditions of the remaining six études of Opus 10 to a muffled background of coughs and throat clearings and nose blowings and candy suckings ineffectually suppressed, hearing aids pinging off along with occasional insolent show-off attempts at applause meant to mark the end of an étude greeted by Plaszcynski each time with a hiss—Idiot! Relentlessly he went on playing, pausing only for a moment before diving into No. 12, "Revolutionary," the last étude of Opus 10, to announce, "We proceed immediately to Opus 25. No intermission. Guards, lock da doors!"

He barked out a laugh, turning to acknowledge me for the first time that evening as if to ascertain if I had appreciated his joke in all its contextual allusiveness, calling unwanted attention to me with a demonic grimace, then plunged immediately into his extended version of the first étude of Opus 25, "Aeolian Harp"—Our song, he seemed to be coyly suggesting. Dutifully, I had continued getting up to turn the pages throughout his performance, because that's what I had been hired to do, that is what I was by training, a page turner, a professional, it was my job, though it was obvious he didn't need me, he wasn't even looking at the music, he was casting his black looks at the audience, punctuating his performance with a periodic "Shot op!"—and truth be told, making many mistakes in his playing, some surprisingly elementary. Now, though, by publicly communicating with me, and thereby confirming my existence, I could sense his intention to out me, to puncture my invisibility and suck me in, to recycle me from bystander to collaborator.

I had what seemed like endless sitting time up there because of the protracted tempo with which he was holding us captive, time to discreetly glance around the hall at the shrinking audience, at those miserable refugees who were still trying to escape, bent over, praying not to be noticed, Plaszcynski mumbling in Polish, "Go already, imbecile, go!"—without pausing a minute from attacking the keyboard. But on the faces of those of us who dutifully remained hostage in our assigned seats and stuck it out was the strain of projecting our best concert behavior, assuming a posture and look that identified us as intelligent, informed, reverent listeners, cultured members of the human race of whom the maestro would approve, my mother's face perhaps most painfully contorted by the effort to please this expired wunderkind. That was the most pathetic thing of all—we wanted Plaszcynski to think well of us, to like us. My father, meanwhile, situated front row center beside my mother, amused himself with some air conducting at the beginning of the first étude of Opus 25, then fell asleep with his chin tucked into his chest and his mouth dropped open, and began snoring during No. 2, "The Bees," threatening to drown out even Plaszcynski's top volume, his snores growing ever louder despite my mother's pinches, delivered discreetly but mercilessly below the belt so as not to interfere with her rapt look through the next three études, waking up at last with a start at No. 5, "Wrong Note," and inquiring in Polish for all to hear, "Still up there banging, the Polack anti-Semit?"

Unfazed, Plaszcynski slammed into No. 6, "Thirds," and onward, sustaining from one étude to the next his slow motion, top decibel, one-size-fits-all dynamics interpretation, yet even above all that sound, managing to inform the audience in English, "So we make deal. If it kosher for you guys to tawk at concert, I tawk also—okay?"

Carrying on nonstop with his playing but with his head now explicitly turned away from the audience, notably turned away also from the keyboard, full facing just me at his left as if it were now only the two of us in a private chamber, he spotlighted me exclusively as the sole higher life form among the rabble, a worthy vessel in which to pour his elevated discourse. Through the stretched-out amplification of the remaining six études I sat there receiving the stream of his words, I sank all my energy into sitting there properly as I was paid to do, offering no reply, my brain spinning, feeling myself liable any minute to be unmoored by dizziness, my heart beating too loud, too loud, Plaszcynski would hear it, it would irritate him, he would be extremely annoyed, it would turn into a spectacle.

It wasn't the noise or the moving around, Plaszcynski was telling me in Polish, or the program pages turning or the rummaging in purses or the cell phones or the belching or burping or scratching, and so on, that bothered him, no—how could anyone in his right mind even imagine such a thing? Everyone knew he was Plaszcynski, famous for his powers of concentration, for his focus, for his ability to tune out every distraction and disturbance—for that alone, quite apart from his music, he was legendary. There was that concert when someone jumped from the second balcony propelled by the power of the music and broke his neck, sacrificing himself to the sacredness of art, and he, Plaszcynski, did not even notice it when it happened, didn't even blink, didn't notice the commotion, the calls for a doctor in the house, the paramedics, the ambulance guys, nothing, didn't stop playing for a minute, didn't skip a beat as they say, didn't register a thing about it until someone happened to mention it afterward in the dressing room. Another time, some guy in the front row, sitting just about where that old yid is sitting—Plaszcynski jerked the back of his head in the direction of my father—pulled out a knife and stuck it in his heart from pure devotion to art, from his love of the music he stabbed his own body in the very spot where he was feeling its beauty most intensely. Blood was gushing from him in every direction, like from a broken pipe, up onto the stage even, squirting all over my new tuxedo, but did I pay any attention? Of course not, it would never have occurred to me, my head was somewhere else, in the heavenly sphere, I didn't notice what was happening on earth. And if I had noticed, would I have stopped playing? Never. I would have understood the priorities, I would have respected the emotion, I would have appreciated the gesture, I would have honored it by ignoring it. But here in your ridiculous little third-world country, your concert hall doesn't even have a proper balcony for a civilized person overcome with passion to jump from, and because of your fascist security, nobody can even bring a knife into the hall to lay bare the passion in his heart much less file the mushrooms off his toenails—so what's the point? Plaszcynski bopped his head back again toward my father, as if to sympathize with the old man so unjustly deprived of the basic tools for the expression of the most profound aesthetic feelings.

"That old yid sitting there right up in the front row who just now called me anti-Semite?" Plaszcynski, with his fingers digging even harder into the keys and his foot nailed to the pedal, slowing down even more as if he were having trouble talking and playing at the same time, was warming to the rant for my sake alone. "I bet you a million shekels that if we gave that old yid a chance, the next thing that would come out of his old mouth would be that the Poles were even worse than the Germans. Right?"

Yes, right, he was correct, Plaszcynski, that would have been the next sentence, I could have attested to that fact had I been able to speak, but something was blocking my throat, if I had tried to scream, nothing would have come out, though it was even in my power to ease his pain to some degree by offering the consolation, for whatever it was worth, that the old yid—did Plaszcynski know he was my father?—that elderly Jewish gentleman, in making his rankings, would invariably also have added that the Croats were the worst of all, worse even than the Poles, not to mention the Ukrainians, even Hitler had to tell them to take it easy. "Even Chopin they call an anti-Semite—can you believe it?" Plaszcynski pushed on. "So how come Horowitz and Rubinstein loved him so much, tell me that? And what about that old Jewish lady who finally dropped dead at age one hundred and ten who was always being dusted off and propped up by Holocaust central public relations to reminisce how Chopin's music saved her life when she was in Terezin, she was talking about these very études no less—what about her? The Germans dump their shit on our soil and the whole world calls them Polish death camps, as if we did it, as if the camps were our brilliant idea, as if without our full and enthusiastic cooperation they could never have gotten the job done. Is that right, is that fair?"

Plaszcynski stopped speaking, though not pounding, for an instant, awaiting my response, but in vain, I had migrated elsewhere. From the distance, I could hear him now asking me almost plaintively, "What am I doing here in this place playing for these rotting leftovers?"—and without expecting an answer this time, launching immediately into a recitation of the reasons the whole world hates the Jews, why every country tries to get rid of them sooner or later, why the Jews are to blame for all the afflictions that have ever beset humankind, the stale litany growing more and more faint and distant as he was rolling it out and I was floating farther away, carried off so gently into a long dark tunnel, a passageway narrowing like a cone, sloping downward, ending in a black dot, and I so tiny curled up in that black dot, I was nothing but a tiny black dot, I was washed in a feeling of pure serenity, Let me remain here forever, I was thinking, when a great and terrible bang hurled me back, Plaszcynski had finished the last étude of Opus 25: No. 12 in C minor, "Ocean," the waves rising, rising—crashing! He had slammed down the cover over the keyboard, scraped back the bench, and without deigning to turn toward the audience for even a perfunctory bow, marched off the stage to limp applause, mainly from the Polish delegation. I was lying on my back on the floor of the stage, how I had landed there I never knew, my mother at my feet tugging down the hem of my black skirt, calling even more attention to how exposed I was. Looking up, I recognized swarming in all around the mass of familiar old tribal faces from my audience, looming over me, staring down at me freely and unobstructed, all of them screaming at once—their advice, their opinions, their arguments, their commentary, their complaints, their clamoring memories, their eternal discord and noise.

The Third Generation

This was not the first time that the father-and-son team Maurice and Norman Messer, respectively chairman of the board and president of Holocaust Connections, Inc., had traveled home from Poland, but it was definitely the saddest. In all their business dealings for clients they had always come through with flying colors, which was how they had built their enviable reputation and their legendary success. But this time, in a most painful personal matter involving an exceedingly close member of their immediate family, indeed, the very future of their line, they had failed completely. Nekhama only child of an only son, had absolutely refused to see her father or her grandfather, either one on one or in any constellation. In any case, as they were categorically informed, she had taken a vow of silence. This was communicated to the two men by a matronly nun in sunglasses, who came to meet them outside the gate of the Carmelite convent—the new convent, that is, a little farther back from the perimeter of the Auschwitz death camp, to which the nuns had moved after all that fuss. "Sister Consolatia asks that you respect her right to choose," the nun told them with finality, in English, though Maurice of course knew Polish. Hearing the signature phrasing, the Messers, father and son, could not deceive themselves that this was anything other than a direct quotation from their apostate offspring, their lost Nekhama, now reborn as Sister Consolatia.

Nevertheless, despite their unquestionably genuine and heart-breaking disappointment, they made themselves comfortable, as usual, in their ample seats in the first-class compartment of the LOT airplane. They always flew Polish, as a matter of policy, to maintain healthy relations with the government with which they had so many dealings; and they always flew first class, because to do otherwise would be unseemly for men like themselves, steeped as they were in such nearly mythic tragic history, a history that set them apart from ordinary people and therefore required that they be seated apart. And from a practical, business point of view, to go economy would look bad, as if their enterprise were falling on hard times. Everything in their line of work, naturally, hung on image. "Look," as Norman formulated it, with the pauses and swallows that usually heralded the delivery of one of his aphorisms, "we already did cattle cars. From now on it's first class all the way." Clients expected a premium operation from the Messers, and were billed accordingly. This trip, for example, had been paid for by an anti-fur organization that was eager to firm up its honorary Holocaust status, and Norman had managed, even in the midst of his private anguish, to do a little work for them, still in its early stages, admittedly, involving the creative use of the mountains of hair in the Auschwitz museum, shorn from the gassed victims—a ghoulish idea on the face of it, which he was now massaging and dignifying in order to establish the relevant ethical connection that would ennoble the agenda of the fur account and give it that moral stamp of the Holocaust.

By now, of course, father and son knew all the flight attendants on the airline. Maurice persisted in referring to them, politically incorrectly, as "hoistesses," a teasing liberty for which he took the precaution of propitiating them, just in case, with little offerings from the luxury hotels of Warsaw and Krakow—miniature shampoos or scented soaps from the bathrooms, chocolate hearts wrapped in gold foil plucked off the pillows. He squeezed and harassed their vivid blondness and springy buxomness hello and good-bye and thank you, muttering, "Don't worry, girls, don't worry, I'm safe."

"And he gets away with it, too," Norman painstakingly and unnecessarily explained to his wife, Arlene, "because he's this cute little tubby old bald Jewish guy with pudgy hands and a funny accent, and the dumb chicks from Częstochowa, they think he's harmless—big mistake, ladies!—so it turns into your stereotypical Polish joke."

They boarded the plane ahead of the common passengers, wearing to the very last minute their trademark trench coats— the sexy semiotics, as Maurice and Norman interpreted it, of international mystery and intrigue. Then one of the attendants, Magda or Wanda or someone, without even inquiring, her brain imprinted with their preferences as if the storage of such information were her reason for existence, glided forward with a welcoming smile such as had long vanished from their wives' repertoires, bearing in front of her two living and breathing breasts a tray with their usual—for Maurice, a glass of Bordeaux ("I'm a red-wine male," he liked to confide urbanely at official functions), for Norman, rum with Coca-Cola, two containers of chocolate milk, and a dozen bags of honey-roasted peanuts.

For a long time they sat side by side in silence, each with his own thoughts, perfectly at ease with the other, apart yet joined, Norman tearing open with his teeth pack after pack of the peanuts, pouring them out into the ladle of his palm, jiggling them around like dice, and then, with his head tilted slightly back, dumping them into his mouth with a smack. He went on doing this automatically, mechanically. Dispatching the nuts this way was okay when he traveled alongside his father. The old man didn't mind, most likely didn't even notice; like most survivor parents, he probably just registered gratefully that at least his son was eating, and for Norman, it was a stolen pleasure, because this was not a snacking style in which he could ever have indulged had he been with his wife or daughter. That robotic, cranelike up-and-down motion of his arm drove the two of them crazy; they could feel its vibration even if they weren't looking directly at him. Maybe that's why Nekhama went into the convent, Norman speculated—because of his annoying habits.

As for Arlene, well, he was just not going to think about his upcoming meeting with her while he was masticating. He simply refused even to begin to plan how he would manage her on the Nekhama problem when he got home, how he would confirm that, unfortunately, it looked, at least for the time being, as if this nun thing was a done deal. They could do nothing about it for the moment except, of course, to use Arlene's idiom, go on being supportive, love their daughter unconditionally, always be there for her, but, at the same time, they needed to allow time to grieve—figuratively grieve, that is, not actually go into mourning by sitting shiva for seven days, like those ultra-Orthodox fanatics when one of their kids converted—and then, of course, they'd need closure, they'd need to move on with their own lives, to let go of all this bad stuff, put it behind them, give the healing process a chance to work, blah-blah.

"Look at it this way," he could say to Arlene. "The bad news is, it's a fact: she's a nun, so that makes her a Christian, I guess, a goy, a shiksa, even worse, a Catholic. We just have to face it. And also it's a problem, I suppose, that she had to go and pick that Carmelite convent right by Auschwitz, of all places, for her nun phase, where three quarters of our family was incinerated. Know what I mean? On the other hand"—and here he would slow down and suck in air for greater effect—"the good news is, she's safe, she has a guaranteed roof over her head and food to eat every day, guys can't bother her anymore, and, from a parent's point of view, we will now always know exactly where she is at all times."

Hey, he loved the girl as much as Arlene did, Norman thought resentfully. Why was he always the one on the defensive? Did he really need this added grief? Nekhama was his daughter too, for God's sake. This whole mess was no less an embarrassment for him than it was for Arlene. Jesus, this could even impact their business, their lifestyle—you hear that, Mrs. Messer, hel-lo? How was it going to look, he demanded of his wife in his head: "HOLOCAUST HEIRESS DUMPS JEWS"? It was an emergency damage-control situation requiring a rapid response. He had to figure out some way to market this negative to their advantage, to turn it around—something like, you know, the ongoing trauma of the Holocaust, the continuing threat to our survival, the Holocaust is not yet over, et cetera, et cetera.

No problem; he was prepared to deal with it. But there was one thing he wanted to know, just one thing—why was he always the one who had to be, as Arlene would put it, supportive, like some Goddamn jockstrap? Why couldn't she be supportive of him once in a while for a change? Had it penetrated her ozone layer yet that everywhere her poor schlump of a husband went, he was a big man, he was greeted like a hero? Was she cognizant of that fact? In Warsaw the women adored him, especially since he had lost all that weight; but the fact is, over there they had always loved him, they loved him in any shape or form, they loved him for himself. They came up to his hotel room carrying bouquets of flowers and bottles of champagne, with beautifully made-up faces and beautifully sprayed hair, in shiny high-heeled shoes and gorgeous real-leather mini-dresses with exposed industrial-strength steel zippers running from neck to hem—not that he carped the diem, needless to say. In the States they worshipped him, idolized him for his aura of suffering, like a saint, like a holy man out of Dosto-evsky. They revered him for never letting up on this miserable Holocaust business, for immersing himself in it every minute, for schlepping the Shoah around on his back day and night, for sacrificing his happiness to keep the flame going—not for his own health, obviously, but for the moral and ethical health of humankind. The anguish in his eyes, the melancholy in the set of his mouth, the manifest depression in the way he blow-dried his hair, the sorrowful awareness of man's inhumanity to man in the way he belted his trench coat—it turned them on, yes, it turned them on.

So big deal, his wife didn't appreciate him. So what else was new? She was happiest when he was away from home, that was obvious; she was delighted that his job required so much traveling. Fine, he could live with that, too, as long as somebody appreciated him, as long as someone somewhere was glad to see him once in a while and showed him a little respect. But it was another thing entirely to blame him for the whole fiasco. C'mon, was he the one who put the kid in the nunnery? Please! And why was he going home now, of his own free will, to listen to all that garbage? He must be *meshuga*. It was masochism, pure and simple, a sick craving for punishment—he should see a shrink. Did he have any doubts whatsoever about what Arlene was going to dump on him, with her squeegee social worker's brain and her prepackaged psychological explanations? Oh, it was an old song; he had heard it a thousand times already. She would start in again with the whole bloody litany—how it was all his fault, everything that had happened was his fault. Right from the start. First of all, what kind of sick idea was it to insist on naming a baby Nekhama? A poor, innocent baby, to give her a name like Comfort, as in "Comfort ye, comfort ye, oh my people," like some sort of replacement Jew, like some sort of post-catastrophe consolation prize, as if they were all depending on her to make things right again after the disaster. Such a heavy load, such an impossible burden to saddle a kid with—no wonder the poor girl took herself out of this world. Did he think names don't matter? There was a whole literature on the subject, on the effect of names on development and identity and self-image. What kind of father would do such a thing to his own flesh and blood? It was criminal, unforgivable. Why couldn't she have been given a normal name, some sort of hopeful, pursuit-of-happiness American name that people could at least pronounce, like Stacy, or Tracy?

And then this whole second-generation business that he had gotten himself involved with, dragging Nekhama along like some sort of archetypal sacrificial lamb, like Jephthah's daughter, like Iphigenia. As a matter of fact, Norman knew very well that most mental-health types just loved the second-generation concept. They ate it up. But Arlene—surprise, surprise—didn't believe in it at all. Why? It was completely predictable: because it served Norman's agenda, that's why, because it legitimized and explained his obsession, and gave it status. There was nothing in it for Arlene. As far as Arlene was concerned, second generation was a made-up category, an indulgence for a bunch of whiners and self-pitiers with a terminal case of arrested development. The so-called survivors were the first generation; they were the ones who had been there, had experienced it all firsthand, and after them came their children, this bogus second generation, the survivor proxies, these Holocaust hangers-on, Norman and company, throwing a tantrum for a piece of Shoah action. So all those tough, shrewd, paranoid refugees who came out of the war— you don't even want to begin to think about how they made it through—suddenly they get turned into sacred, saintly survivors with unutterable knowledge, and then the second generation, born and reared in Brooklyn or somewhere, far, far from the gas chambers and the crematoria, gets crowned as honorary survivors. Suddenly these lightweight descendants are endowed with gravitas, with importance, with all the seriousness and rewards that come from sucking up to suffering. What could be neater? All the benefits of Auschwitz without having to actually live through that nastiness.

And what did they do to deserve this honor, this second generation? What exactly are their suffering bona fides? Well, they had it rough, poor babies—they are victims too, you can't take it away from them. They suffered the psychic wounds of being raised by traumatized, overprotective parents with impossible expectations. They bore the weight of having to transmit the torch of memory, that kitschy memorial candle, from past to future. They endured a devastating blow to their self-esteem in consequence of the knowledge that their lives were a paltry sideshow compared with their parents' epic stories. It was sick, sick, pathetic—"Holocaust envy," a new term in the profession, coming your way soon in the updated, revised edition of *DSM-IV*. And to think that he would expose his own child to such a pathological situation—to think he'd go ahead now and render this acute condition chronic by prolonging the agony, by trying to pass the whole load on to Nekhama like a life sentence, like indentured servitude, like guilt unto the tenth generation. Was it an accident, then, that she abandoned the Jews for the ultimate martyr religion, complete with vicarious suffering as its main value and a tortured skinny guy on a cross as its main icon? Was it an accident that she found her way back to the gates of Auschwitz? Had it never dawned on him where this morbid Holocaust fixation would lead?

"Maybe we should've come with one of those deprogramming fellas," Maurice was now saying. "Maybe we should've climbed the wall from the convent like that crazy rabbi—what's his name?—when it used to be in the other building where they used to keep the gas in the war. Maybe we should've kidnapped her from the *schwesters.*"

Norman shook his head. "Bad idea, Pop." He swallowed portentously before elaborating. "It would have been disastrous for Polish-Jewish relations, a nightmare for Catholic-Jewish relations, not to mention curtains for business relations."

"Nu. Anyway, you have to be a younger man for that kind of monkey business, climbing walls. You know what I mean? And you're not so young anymore, Normie, ha ha, and I'm not in such good shape—like your mama says, svelte. I'm not so svelte like I used to be when I was a leader from the partisans and fought against the Nazis in the woods."

Norman had to catch his breath and squeeze the bridge of his nose to stem the keen rush of longing for his daughter that swept over him at that moment, as Maurice recited the familiar refrain in exactly those words about having been a partisan leader who fought the Nazis in the woods. It was a private joke between Norman and Nekhama. They would mouth those exact words every time Maurice uttered them, flawlessly imitating his grimaces and gestures, mouth them behind the old man's back at gatherings with friends and family or even at the public speeches that he regularly gave in synagogues, community centers, and schools about his career as a resistance fighter, which he always began with the sentence "I'm here to debunk the myth that the Jews went like sheep to the shlaughter." Norman and Nekhama would mouth this sentence, too, in fits of choking, mute hilarity. It was a harmless father-daughter ritual that had started when she was about eighteen or nineteen years old, after Maurice had given his standard talk, at Nekhama's invitation, in her college's Jewish students' center, opening, as usual, with that sentence about the sheep-to-the-slaughter myth, and ending, as usual, by snapping smartly to attention when they played the Partisans' Hymn, "Never Say That You Have Reached the Final Road."

In a moment alone with Nekhama during the reception following Maurice's talk, the two of them facing each other with their clear plastic wineglasses filled with sparkling cider, as if playing a couple just introduced at a social gathering, Norman casually mentioned—in another context entirely, he forgot what—that of course nobody really knew exactly what Maurice Messer had done during the Holocaust except that he had hidden in the woods all day and stolen chickens at night. No shame in that, of course, under the circumstances. "You just gotta face it, kiddo," Norman went on, in the grip of something beyond his control, "he never shot in the woods—he shat in the woods!"

"You mean Grandpa wasn't really a partisan leader who fought the Nazis?" The child seemed genuinely shocked.

Norman raised an eyebrow. His daughter was not being ironic. Maybe he had gone too far this time. Maybe she really was an innocent; maybe she was just too fragile for this kind of realpolitik. Incredibly, it looked as if she truly hadn't fathomed until that moment that her grandfather's story was just an innocuous piece of self-promoting fiction. But when, after a long pause to absorb the new information, she mischievously blurted out, "Okay, Dad, I won't be the one to tell the Holocaust deniers that it's all made up," he breathed again with relief, impressed by how quickly she had caught on, how alert she was to where her interests lay and her loyalties belonged, how sophisticated she was in accepting human weakness as another amusing fact of life.

"Look," Norman intoned, "it's not as if he didn't really suffer. You think it's easy being considered a victim all the time, having people feel sorry for you—especially if you're a macho type like Grandpa? Who's going to be hurt by an old man's little screenplay starring himself as the big hero? Tell me that, please." He slowed down emphatically now to make way for the flourish. "The Holocaust market is not about to collapse due to one old man's inflations, trust me. Those loonies who say the whole thing never happened should not take comfort."

Should not take comfort, he had said—not take *nekhama*. Anyway, it was from that time on, as he recalled it, that they engaged in their tradition of delicious mockery, all in affectionate fun, whenever Maurice warmed up and delivered his partisan spiel. It had evolved into their own personal father-daughter thing. And it was the memory of this innocent conspiratorial bonding with his child that took possession of him now and overcame him.

"Nu, Normie," Maurice was saying. "Yes or no? Why you not talkin'? You remember that hoo-hah with the *schwesters* at the convent with that crazy rabbi, like your mama calls him?"

Maurice, whenever possible, liked to quote his wife, to whom he gallantly conceded a superior mastery of English idiom and pronunciation, and whom he regarded as a nearly oracular source of common sense. For example, whenever the subject came up of that rabbi who had caused an international incident with his protest against the presence of a Catholic convent at Auschwitz, where a million Jews had been gassed—the very same convent in which, in a more acceptable location ordained by the pope himself, their granddaughter Nekhama was now a nun praying for the salvation of the souls of the Jewish dead—Blanche would open her eyes wide and exclaim, "But, darling, he's crazy!" In consequence, Maurice never failed, when referring to that event at the old Carmelite convent, to include the epithet "that crazy rabbi"—as if the rabbi's mental state were a genuine clinical diagnosis, because Blanche, with her peerless common sense, had declared it to be so. Common sense, in Maurice's opinion, was an exceedingly desirable quality in a woman, and there was a time when he had advised Norman to put it at the top of his list of qualities in choosing a mate. To which Blanche would always remark coyly, "When they tell you a girl has common sense, that's a code for not so ay-yay-yay—in other words, not so pretty." "Common sense together with pretty," Maurice would then chime in with alacrity, "just like mine Blanchie."

They discussed everything, he and Blanche, even the subjects they did not discuss. They discussed but did not discuss, for instance, their shared sense of the limitations of their Norman's capabilities. It was not an understanding that they cared to seal in words. But around the time they sold their ladies'-undergarments company, Messers' Foundations, from which they had made a more than comfortable living, the Holocaust had become fashionable, more fashionable even than padded brassieres and spandex girdles. At first the two of them had booked up their retirement by becoming leaders in the survivor community and popular lecturers on the oral-testimony circuit. The Holocaust was hot, no question about it. Blanche then urged Maurice to start the consulting business, Holocaust Connections, Inc., and to take Norman in as an equal partner. "Make Your Cause a Holocaust," as their smart-aleck Norman packaged it; he was just too much. It would be first and second generation working and playing together, an ideal setup, a perfect outlet for their Norman, the original futzer and putzer, as they lovingly called him, whose jobs until then, they agreed, had been totally beneath him, totally unsatisfactory and unchallenging. Now Norman could hang around all day long, talking creatively with clients on the telephone, holding forth with all his brilliant opinions, cracking his wicked jokes, writing an article now and then for a Jewish newspaper, traveling and schmoozing in diplomatic channels and the corridors of power with all the other politicians and insiders—the best possible use of his considerable gifts and talents. Unspoken was their shared sense that Norman needed their help, that fundamentally he was a weak person, that he could never manage on his own. Never mind that he had gone to Princeton University— Princeton, Shminceton!—where he had even taken part in a sit-in in the president's office for three days and nights, though his mother had marched right into the middle of that nonstop orgy to personally hand him his allergy medicine. Never mind that he had a law degree from Rutgers, where they trained poor schlemiels to become a bunch of creepers and crawlers. Never mind that he was an adult, to all appearances a grown man, with a social-worker wife and a beautiful but moody daughter. They knew in their hearts that if the war broke out tomorrow, their Norman would never make it. Without saying it out loud, they recognized that, unlike themselves, Norman would not have survived.

Survival—that was the bottom line. You couldn't argue with it. It was the fact on the ground that separated the living from the dead. That was the lesson they had struggled to drum into their Norman: first you survive, then you worry about such niceties as morality and feelings. When someone tells you he's going to kill you, you pay attention, you take him seriously, you believe him. You wake up earlier the next morning and you kill him. If you survive, you win. If you don't survive, you lose. If you lose, you're nothing. What is Rule No. 1 for survival? Never trust anyone. Suspect everyone. Take it as a given that the other guy is out to destroy you, and eat him alive before he gets the chance. Why had they survived? Luck, they always said. It was luck. But they didn't believe it for a minute. It was the accepted thing to say, so as not to insult the memory of the ones who hadn't survived, the ones who were now piles of gray ash and crushed bone that people stepped on. The real truth, they knew, was that they had survived because they were stronger, better—fitter. Look at the survivors today, the ones who had staggered out of the camps like the living dead. They were your classic greenhorns, eternal immigrants, afraid to offend by harping on the Holocaust—why make a federal case of it?—a bunch of nobodies until they had their consciousness raised by the survivor elite, by Blanche and Maurice's circle, the ones who survived with style, the fearless ones. "Me? I'm never afraid!" Maurice always said. It was his motto. Now, thanks to them, the Holocaust was a household word. They built monuments and museums. They were millionaires, big shots, movers and shakers. They ran the country. Survival of the fittest. Blanche had once read in a magazine that cancer cells were the fittest form of life, because they ate everything else up, they spread, they reproduced, they survived, they won. Maybe this wasn't such a wonderful example; maybe this didn't reflect so nicely on her and Maurice and the rest—to be compared to cancer. Cancer was bad, but in this world if you survive, you win, and if you win, you're good.

They were a formidable team, Blanche and Maurice Messer, a fierce couple, and proud of it. For their fortieth wedding anniversary Norman and Arlene had given them a plaque engraved with the words "Don't Mess with the Messers," which they hung in "Holocaust Central," their den off the living room, right above the composition that Nekhama had written when she was eight years old, in third grade. The topic was "My Hero"; Nekhama had chosen Maurice.

Grandpa had a gun in World War II. He killed bad Germans with the gun. He was a Germ killer. He saved the Jewish people. He loved the gun. He kissed the gun good-night every night. He slept with the gun. After the war they gave Grandpa a ride on a tank. He was holding the gun. Then they took the gun away. Grandpa was sad. He cried because he missed his gun. So he married Grandma.

The teacher gave her only a "Fair" for this effort, but Blanche said, "What does she know? It's not by accident that she's a teacher," and she hung the composition, expensively framed, on the wall. "I'm the gun," she asserted defiantly. Maurice also didn't care much for this composition. "What for is she telling the *ganze velt* this partisan story? It's private, just for family." "What are you worrying about, Maurie?" Blanche said. "Every survivor is a partisan. Survival is resistance." "Don't be so paranoid, Pop," Norman said. "It's safe to come out of the closet now." Then, swallowing deliberately and pausing pregnantly, he added, "Ziggy and Manny and Feivel and Yankel, and everyone else who was with you in the woods in those days, they're all dead by now, may they rest in peace—and quiet."

Again, it was a question of survival, this time the survival of the Jewish people in an age of assimilation and intermarriage and the mixed-blessing decline of anti-Semitism in America— another Holocaust, frankly, even more dangerous in its way, because it was insidious, underground. Blanche and Maurice would do anything to ensure Jewish survival. No effort or sacrifice was too great, and, as they knew very well, nothing could compare to the Holocaust for bagging a straying Jew; it was the best seller, it was the top of the line, it got the customer every time. Why did God give us the Holocaust? For one reason only: to drive home the lesson that once a Jew, always a Jew. You could try to blend in and fade out, you could try to mix and match, but it was all useless, hopeless. There was no place to hide, no way to run. Hitler would find you wherever you were and flush you out like a cockroach.

And what could be more effective in sending this message loud and clear than a partisan leader and his wife—herself a survivor of three death camps, maybe four, depending on how you counted—telling their story over and over again until they were blue in the face, pounding in nonstop, day and night, the lessons of the Holocaust. Whatever it took to beat in the message, even if it meant pushing themselves into the limelight in crude ways that ran thoroughly counter to their refined nature, even if it meant giving the misleading impression that they were exploiting the dead, they would do it, not for personal fame and glory, God forbid, but for the cause, because this was their mission. This was why they had been chosen. This was the reason they had survived. They were the first generation, the eyewitnesses. Norman was the connecting link. Nekhama was continuity.

Yes, continuity. She was their designated kaddish, their living memorial candle, the third generation. And now she was a Christian. This was tragic—tragic! How could it have happened? Who could ever have foreseen such an outcome? It was beyond human imagining. They had thrown everything they had into that girl. She had always been the ideal apprentice and protégé. She was, as Maurice used to say in his speeches, the spitting image of his mother, Shprintza Chaya Messer the guerrilla fighter, shot down by the Nazis during the roundup in Wieliczka while she screamed at the top of her lungs, "Fight, Yidalekh, fight!"

To this day people still talked about Nekhama's bat mitzvah speech—how she had turned to address the ghost of the Vilna girl with whom she had insisted on being twinned with the words "Rosa, my sister, you were cruelly cut down by the Nazis during the Holocaust. You never had a bat mitzvah. Today I give back to you what was so wrongfully taken away—because today I am you." Arlene, with her naïve American Oh-say-can-you-see attitude, had called this gruesome, morbid, a form of child abuse, and had walked out of the sanctuary, but everyone else felt spiritually uplifted and morally renewed by Nekhama's words, and wept contentedly. And who could forget the Holocaust assemblies that Nekhama had organized in high school, at which either Maurice or Blanche gave testimony? Once even Norman, as the ambassador of the second generation, addressed the teenagers, with their yellow paper stars for Jews pinned to their Nine Inch Nails T-shirts, their pink triangles for homosexuals, black triangles for Gypsies. Especially, who could forget Nekhama's original dance composition, presented each year, "Requiem for the Absent," with the flowing, twisting scarves and the arms reaching poignantly toward the heavens? She had always been so proud of her family, those Holocaust relics who would have mortified your average adolescent, and had even invited her grandparents and her father to accompany her to Poland for the March of the Living, with thousands of other Jewish girls and boys from all over the world—but she was in a class apart. She was a Holocaust princess. And she wasn't ashamed of the VIP treatment that she received because of her family's position in the Holocaust hierarchy, and she wasn't embarrassed to walk at a slower pace alongside the old folks for the three-kilometer march from Auschwitz to the actual killing center in Birkenau, with its remains of gas chambers and crematoria, and ash and powdered bone underfoot. She had turned to them and said—they would never forget it—"I see them, I hear them, I feel them. The dead are walking beside us." And then, in her essay for her college application, she had written, "The one thing about me that you may or may not have learned so far from this application is that I am, in the most positive and constructive sense, a Holocaust nut. What this means is that I am totally obsessed by the Holocaust, the murder of six million of my people, and am determined to do everything in my power to make sure that these dead shall not have died in vain." "Beautiful, beautiful," Maurice had declared, "like the Star-Spangled Banana!" She was rejected by Princeton, even though she was legacy, because deep down they were, as Maurice put it, "a bunch of anti-Semitten and shtinkers." So she went to Brown.

With such Holocaust credentials, who would ever have predicted that she would turn her back on her people and become, of all things, a nun? Convent and continuity—these were two concepts that definitely did not go together. They did not mix well. They were not a natural couple. The idea of a nun was very foreign to Jewish thinking. Among Jews every girl got married one way or another, every girl had children, and if one didn't— well, that just never happened. Who ever heard of such a thing? Ever since she was a little girl, she had talked so movingly about how she would have at least twelve children to help make up for the millions who had been murdered—hurled alive into flaming pits, shot, gassed, their heads bashed against stone walls. She was going to be a baby machine for Jewish continuity. She was a pretty girl, everyone remarked—a little full, maybe. "Zaftig," Maurice said. "Baby fat," Blanche said. Her favorite food, according to family lore, was marzipan, and even that preference was regarded as a sign of her superiority. It was so European, so Old World—what ordinary American Mars Bars kid knows from marzipan? The boys who were attracted to her were usually considerably older, usually foreigners. One of the family's favorite stories was about how she had stayed out very late one night, and when she finally came home, at five in the morning, her excuse to her worried parents was that this Salvadoran guy named Salvador had asked her out, and she didn't want to hurt his feelings, so she had to explain to him that she could never date a non-Jew, because of the Holocaust—it was nothing personal, but her duty was to replace the six million. And then, of course, she had to tell him the whole history of the Holocaust, so that he'd understand where she was coming from—starting with Hitler's rise to power, in 1933, and continuing to the end of World War II, in 1945, which took a long time. Which was why she was so late. She hoped they weren't mad. "So what did Salvador say?" Norman had asked, obviously not mad at all, obviously gratified. "Oh, he said, 'I only asked you out for a cup of coffee. I didn't ask you to marry me.' But that's not the point."

And she never did date a non-Jew, so far as they knew. In any case, soon after she entered college, her romantic life became a mystery to them, off limits as a subject. She did, it is true, bring home a number of gentile boys, but this was "purely platonic," as she put it—"We're just friends." She knew them in connection with her activities to end the persecution of Christians throughout the world. "A Christian Holocaust is going on as we speak," she declared at dinner in the presence of one of these guests, "and as a Jew who could have been turned into a lampshade, I cannot in good conscience remain a silent bystander." She brought home a Chinese graduate student who described how he had been beaten and tortured because of his membership in an underground church. She brought home a Sudanese lab technician whose family members had been burned or sold into slavery for practicing their faith. As they narrated their stories at the table, she listened raptly, her eyes moist, her mouth slightly open, even though she had surely heard them before. "Any guy who wants her will have to show torture marks," Arlene said. "What for is she foolin' with the Christians?" Maurice complained to Norman. "Where you think Hitler got all his big ideas from about the Jews, tell me that. And the pope, you should excuse me, His Holiness, where was he during the war—playing pinochle?" "They're trying to hijack the Holocaust," Norman wailed. "Christians are not—I repeat, not!—acceptable Holocaust material. This is where we draw the line."

They tried to wean her from this new fixation by offering her a partnership in their business—complete control of the Women's Holocaust portfolio: abortion, sexual harassment, female genital mutilation, rape, the whole gamut—but she wasn't buying. "The Christians are the new Jews," she said. "Christians have a right to a Holocaust too. Since when do Jews have a monopoly? That's the problem with Jews. They never share." So they broke down after all and offered to take on the Christian Holocaust as part of their business, however alien and distasteful it was to them—to have her create and head up, in fact, a new department devoted entirely to this area. "Forget it," she said. "You guys are too compromised and politicized for me. You'd sell out the victims for the first embassy dinner invitation."

The last time any member of the family had seen her was a few days after she called to say that she would be entering the Carmelite convent near Auschwitz as a postulant, and because it was a contemplative, enclosed, "hermit" order, she would not be available much afterward for visitors. She insisted that though she would soon become a novice and then eventually take vows, she would always consider herself to be a Jewish nun. They should keep that in mind. They were not losing her. They should not despair. The family decided that Arlene would go alone to see her. She accepted the mission despite her frequently voiced resolve never to set foot in that "huge cemetery called Poland—it's no place for a live Jew; this back-to-the-shtetl nostalgia is obscene; these grand tours of the death camps are grotesque." The day after Nekhama called, Arlene flew to Warsaw.

When Nekhama had converted to Catholicism, she had told them that it was a necessary step toward the fulfillment of her "vocation" but they should know and understand that, like the first Christians, she remained also a Jew. "What you mean?" Maurice had demanded. "Are you with us or against us? Are you a goy or a Jew? You can't have it both ways. You can't have your kishke and eat it also!" Norman wanted to know if this was some kind of Jews-for-Jesus deal, but no, she said, it was in the best tradition of the early Church fathers. Norman then made the hopeful point to the family that nowadays maybe you could be both a Christian and a Jew, just as you could, as everyone knew, be both a Buddhist and a Jew—"a Jew-Bude" it was called, something pareve, nothing to get excited about, neither milk nor meat.

Even so, her conversion was a devastating blow, though not entirely unexpected, given her increasing immersion in the Christian Holocaust. After college she had worked full time for the cause at its Washington headquarters, and then had set out on what she called her "pilgrimage," her "crusade," to bear witness to the persecution firsthand at the actual sites throughout the world, and to offer comfort and strength to the oppressed. She had been kicked out of Pakistan for agitation and promoting disorder. In Ethiopia she had been arrested, and major string-pulling had been required to spring her, which, fortunately, her family was able to manage discreetly, thanks to its position in the world and its fancy connections in high places ("A little schmear here, a little kvetch there," as Maurice recounted with satisfaction). As it became clearer and clearer to them that she was heading toward conversion, Norman had tried to make the case to her that she was far more useful to the Christian Holocaust as a Jew, that her Jewishness was an extremely effective media hook. It piqued people's curiosity—what was a nice Jewish girl like her doing in a place like this? It made her far more interesting and, let's face it, bizarre, especially as she was so Jewishly identified, with her family so prominent in Holocaust circles, bringing even greater attention and visibility to the cause. "Besides," Norman added deliberately, "you don't have to be Christian to love the Christian Holocaust. When I do the Whale Holocaust, do I become a whale? Think about it, Nekhama'le. Think again, baby."

From contacts in Poland they knew almost immediately when Nekhama had arrived there. She began a slow circuit of the main extermination camps, stopping for a few days at each one to fast and pray—first Treblinka, then Chelmno, Sobibor, Majdanek, Belzec, until she came, finally, to Auschwitz-Birkenau. She called home to say that she had lit a memorial candle in front of the Carmelite convent for a "blessed Jewish nun," Saint Edith Stein, "Sister Teresa Benedicta of the Cross," Nekhama called her, who was martyred in the gas chambers there. "Oy vey," Maurice had said. "She's talkin' about that convert Edit' Shtein? I'm not feelin' so good!" In another telephone conversation she had made the comment that traditional Judaism provides no real outlet for a woman's spirituality. "I mean, suppose a Jewish woman wants to dedicate her whole heart and soul and all of her strength to loving God and to prayer. Where is there a Jewish convent for that? Does Judaism even acknowledge the existence of a woman's spirituality in any context other than home and family?" She took a room in Oswiecim to be near the nuns. "They're such holy, holy women, it's humbling and uplifting, both at once. How could anyone ever accuse them of trying to Christianize Auschwitz? It's just ridiculous. Everything they do they do out of love."

Nekhama arranged to have Arlene meet her at the large cross near the now-abandoned old convent, the building in which, during the Holocaust, the canisters of Zyklon B gas with which the Jews were asphyxiated had been stored, just at the edge of the death camp. She was already there, praying on her knees, when Arlene's car drove up. Arlene asked the driver to wait for her; she had no intention whatsoever of visiting the camp. After she finished with Nekhama, she would go directly back to Krakow. She would be in Warsaw by evening. She would be on a plane flying out of this cursed country the next morning. As she approached the cross with her daughter kneeling before it, she could see two nuns in full habit posted in the distance. Nekhama herself was wearing an unfamiliar sort of rough garment—probably some sort of nun's training outfit, Arlene thought.

Nekhama heard Arlene approaching, and with her back still turned she signaled with her thumb and index finger rounded into a circle—a gesture she had picked up during a teen trip to Israel—for her mother to wait a few seconds more as she finished her devotions. Then, after placing her lips directly on the wood of the cross and kissing it passionately, she rose to her feet. "Mommy," she cried, and she ran to embrace her mother.

Arlene shocked herself by breaking down in racking sobs that swept over her like a flash storm. Her mascara streaked down her cheeks.

"I'm sorry, I'm sorry," she kept on repeating.

"What are you sorry about? Go on, cry. Crying is good for you—it cleanses the spirit. There's nothing to be ashamed of."

"I'm sorry for letting them screw you up," Arlene sputtered into the coarse cloth of Nekhama's garment. She had not planned to begin this way, but she could not stop herself now. "I'm sorry for not fighting harder to keep them from poisoning you with their Holocaust craziness. I should have fought them like a lioness protecting her cub. They crippled you, crippled you, they destroyed any chance you might have had to lead a normal life—and I did nothing to prevent it."

"Mom?" Nekhama pushed Arlene to arm's length. "Two things, Mom. Number one, I'm not screwed up, and number two, the Holocaust, believe it or not, is the best thing that has ever happened to me. It has made me what I am today. I'm proud of what I am. I'm doing vital, redemptive work. I'm bringing healing to the world. Do you understand? I don't want you to pathologize me—okay, Mom? I'm not a sicko."

Wiping her eyes with a tissue that she held clutched in her fist, Arlene now took the time to look closely at her daughter. Nekhama's face, framed by a kerchief that concealed all of her thick, curly hair, her best feature, was exposed and clear—no makeup, and no sign either of the acne that had distressed her well into her twenties. So convents are good for the complexion, Arlene concluded bitterly. Instead of contact lenses she was wearing glasses with translucent pale-pink plastic frames. The expression in her eyes was serene and benevolent—too placid, Arlene thought; she looked drugged, brainwashed, dead to life. A faint moustache lay over her top lip; in her new life of poverty, chastity, and obedience, in her tight schedule between Lauds and Compline, there was no place for the facial bleaching that Arlene had taught her as part of the beauty regimen of every dark-haired woman. Around her neck was a daunting cross made from some base metal. The womanly fullness of her barren hips bore down earthward against her skirts, pulled down inevitably by gravity whether they fulfilled their biological function or not, Arlene could see. She had put on a little weight—not that it mattered anymore. At least she was getting enough to eat.

Nekhama quickly sensed her mother's appraising eye, and for a moment she was seized by a familiar irritation that she recognized from those times in the past when her mother had rated her appearance down to the last fraction of an ounce and had registered mute disappointment. By an act of will Nekhama shook off this feeling, which she considered unworthy and a vanity.

"You look nice," Arlene finally said. She avoided Nekhama's eyes, gazing up instead at the twenty-six-foot wooden cross looming behind them. "So this is the famous cross that the Jews and the Poles are beating up on each other about."

"Yes—isn't it silly?" Nekhama said. "I guess I'll just never understand what Jews have against a cross."

The Crusades. The Inquisition. Pogroms. Blood libels. The Holocaust. If she can't figure out what we have against the cross, Arlene thought, especially when it is planted right in this spot, where a million Jews were gassed and burned, then she has strayed a long, long way from home. She has gone very far indeed. She is lost to us.

"I mean," Nekhama went on, "what everyone has to realize now, if we're ever going to get beyond this, is that each Jew who was murdered in the Holocaust is another Christ crucified on the cross. When I pray to Him, I pray to each one of them. I pray every day to each of the six million Christs."

Suffering and salvation. Martyrdom and redemption. This was not a language that Arlene recognized. The cross cast its long dark shadow over them and onto the blood-soaked ground beyond. The afternoon was passing. Arlene adjusted the strap of the stylish black-leather bag on her shoulder and glanced toward the waiting car. More than anything else in the world now, she wanted to get away from here, from this madness that bred more madness, from this alien sacred imagery that justified unspeakable atrocities. She wanted ordinariness, dailiness, routine—plans, schedules, menus, lists, programs, things, material goods. "Do you need anything, Nekhama?" Arlene asked. "I mean, before I go—like underwear, vitamins, toiletries? Tell me what you need, and I'll see that you get it."

"Oh, I don't need anything anymore. I'm finished with needing things," Nekhama said, breaking her mother's heart. "We live very simply here. Other people have needs. They send us long lists of what they need, and we pray for them. That's what we do. I can pray for you, too, Mommy. Tell me what you need."

What did she need? She needed to think and see clearly. She needed to remember everything she had forgotten—or she would soon lose faith that she had ever existed at all. "I need to have you back with me," Arlene said quietly, in the voice she would use when she lay down in bed beside her daughter at night, to ease the child into sleep.

Nekhama smiled rapturously. "We'll pray for you," she said, and her glance moved from her mother and the cross above them to encompass her whole world, the two nuns motionless in the distance, and the million dead inside the camp who never rested.

Dedicated to the Dead

Not long after Jack Gallagher realized that, in his previous life, he had been the Jew Yankel Galitzianer, murdered during the war in one of the death camps of Poland, he changed his name to Jacob Gilguli to affirm his reincarnated state, and set out to Jerusalem to find himself. His girlfriend at the time, Bathsheba Finkelkraut, a former drill sergeant in the Israeli army of a physical type to which he had always been guiltily drawn—full-bodied with mighty thighs and a visible mustache, a type in which he indulged as a secret vice unsuitable to his Wall Street connections and Episcopalian bloodline—accompanied him on this first stage of his journey of self-renewal. She was the one, after all, who had guided him to the insight that he was the *gilgul* of Yankel Galitzianer when she showed him an ad in a Hebrew newspaper, a language he could at that point neither read nor understand, for the New Jersey burial society of the Polish shtetl of Przemysl, offering plots to fellow survivors. Immediately he recited the names and described down to the last detail the physical characteristics of his two boyhood comrades, Jacek Lustiger and Henryk Pfefferkorn, who had escaped into the forest three days before the roundups in the town, while he, Yankel Galitzianer, had been herded with whips into a cattle car by black-booted guards, and he rode for a week on the rails in darkness without water or food and nowhere to relieve himself decently until he arrived at a death camp—which camp it was, he could not yet specify— where his fate was to be gassed and cremated. For Jacob Gilguli, this was the absolute recognition of who he was that he had been seeking all his life; not for one minute did he doubt its truth. It fully explained his recurrent nightmares featuring the lashing of whips and high polished black-leather jackboots and sealed freight cars packed with wailing women and children, and yes, men too, young and old, weighed down with pathetic bundles and satchels, and it clarified, too, his lifelong obsession with Holocaust movies such as *Ilsa: She-Wolf of the SS* and others, which were included in his personal collection and which he would flick on at four in the morning as he lay naked in the darkness between the crisp white sheets of his platform bed in his Tribeca loft, his heart pounding, startled into wakefulness by his terrifying dreams.

In Jerusalem, he let his lank blond hair grow long, parted in the middle like two curtains flounced on either side to present his face with its strong horizontals and vertical—the parallel lines of his thin lips and long eyebrows, the straight drop of his refined nose. His beard came in almost platinum in color, coiled and sparse—"Like your poobic hair," Bathsheba commented as she wove her raw fingers through it in bed one night in the room he had taken at the King David Hotel. Soon after, as the last service he required of her, Bathsheba located a shop for him operated by a Muslim known as Abu Shahid, which specialized in outfitting fresh recruits and returnees to the Jewish faith. Gilguli made his way there through the Damascus Gate, into the winding alleyways and arcades of the shuk of the walled Old City. At Abu Shahid's, he bought without haggling a long white cotton tunic manufactured in India, matching loose white drawstring trousers, brown leather Old Testament sandals, and a fringed garment to pull over his shirt like a double-sided bib, with a cluster of silken strings in each of its four corners threaded with celestial blue that lit up the pale blueness of his eyes. To cover his head, he selected a large, close-fitting skullcap crocheted in shades of red, to which he affixed, with small, fine stitches, a yellow star with the word "Jude" inscribed on it that he acquired from Abu Shahid's exclusive private collection of genuine Holocaust relics at a staggering cost, though the merchant, placing hand over heart, swore over and over again on the life of his mother that he was practically giving it away. Even so, despite this economic setback, still unable to resist, he accessorized with a small shofar, which he spotted in a dusty heap in a corner and which, right there in Abu Shahid's stall, he raised to his lips to let out a shattering blast without straining at all, thanks to years of French horn lessons that were among the fringe benefits of his entitled upbringing. All of these items, as well as his room at the King David, he paid for with money from his trust fund, established about a century after his ancestors stepped onto American soil, and which, to his glee, his family could not touch even in the face of their severe disapproval of the unexpected trajectory his career had taken. The yellow Jude badge was his second most costly purchase after the white donkey with its luminous Persian-rug saddlebags, which he acquired from a cousin of Abu Shahid's, and upon which he made his way around the city of Jerusalem and its environs, stabling it at night in special quarters established by the municipality for the white donkeys of other penitents, the self-proclaimed messiahs and the newly enlightened. Yet, notwithstanding this carefully considered equipage and the serious financial outlays it entailed, inevitably, every single Israeli he met would in short order inquire, with a jolting brazenness to which he was entirely unaccustomed by class or breeding, if he was really a Jew—that is, a Jew by birth. And even as he struggled to explain the complicated proposition that his lineage was even purer and more aristocratic than that, that he was a Jew by pre-birth, they would smirk knowingly and smugly proclaim, "I knew it, you definitely don't look Jewish, I could tell right away." There was simply nothing he could do to convince them. This was a stubborn, ill-mannered, arrogant, obnoxious lot he had fallen in among, but what could he do? It was his karma to be one of them.

It had also been through Bathsheba, albeit indirectly, that he had the rare privilege of meeting the legendary holy man and guru Shmuel Himmelhoch, who, according to knowledgeable sources, took upon himself extraordinary acts of penance for what must have been spectacular sins in a cave outside the walls of the city, near Absalom's tomb. Gilguli was astride his white donkey coming up from the direction of Hezekiah's tunnel and the pool of Siloam, with Bathsheba pacing sullenly some distance behind him as he had been obliged to demand due to the unseemly and immodest and, it might also be noted, unbecoming costume of tight khaki shorts and plunging halter top she insisted it was her right to wear, which reflected so negatively upon him, so discredited his mission, so compromised him in his new emanation. Not surprisingly, two Arab boys, justifiably concluding her to be loose and available, leapt from the crags to grab the choicest parts. And though Bathsheba would have been fully capable of dispatching them thanks to her rigorous training in the elite Israel Defense Forces, at that moment Himmelhoch in his spectral white robes, his wild unshorn hair and beard flying, emerged from his cave, waving one arm in agitation while screwing his other hand against his ear in what looked to be intense spiritual pain, startling the boys like crows off a carcass and scattering them in horror. Gilguli and Bathsheba watched in awed silence from their respective stations as Himmelhoch completed his labors—Gilguli insisted afterward that there was no question that the holy man was in ardent communication with the One Above—removed his cell phone from his ear, glared at it reproachfully, and shook it in resignation before turning to enter once again the enveloping dead zone of his cave.

The first words that Himmelhoch spoke to him were in the form of numbers—167277. This happened after months during which Gilguli sat in the cave at the feet of the sage six days a week not including the Sabbath, dredging up from his very depths all of the woes and longings and griefs that oppressed his heart and soul, to be answered only with a weighty silence laced with subtext. Gilguli did not immediately realize that when Himmelhoch uttered those first words his intention was to pass on to his disciple his cell phone number, with the implicit suggestion that Gilguli might save himself a trip and spare his donkey the rocky climb simply by telephoning to continue his outpourings, even unburdening himself into the answering machine should he, Himmelhoch, not be available to take the call. Those first sounds coming directly to his ears from the mouth of the holy man shocked Gilguli for their precious rarity, they hit him as so auspicious and resonant that he instantly knew them to be the numbers that had been branded into his forearm in his past life, when he was the Jew Yankel Galitzianer. That very day he took the bus to Tel Aviv, to a tattoo parlor on Shenkin Street, and submitted himself once again to the ordeal as, in the very molecules of his being beyond time, he remembered having been forced to submit when he was a prisoner in the death camp. It is true that he also had another tattoo, at the summit of his natal crease, acquired in his Gallagher life, during his last year at St. Paul's after a long wretched night of beer and despair—the image of a heart dripping blood pierced by a sword with the name Morgan carved into the hilt. Where was Morgan now? At Bloomingdale's, no doubt, shopping in intimate wear. Of that tattoo he was ashamed, it goes without saying, but of this one on his forearm he remained defiantly proud. He believed with a full faith that someday soon it would be irrefutably shown that, through the collision of mystical forces, the holy man's number was one and the same as his own when he was the doomed slave Yankel Galitzianer, and that through this miraculous confluence of digits a direct line to God was unfurled.

Then one day Himmelhoch took two metal sticks that had been propped in an alcove of his cave and led Gilguli out into the blinding sunlight. Gripping a stick in each gnarled fist by its curved cane-like handle and straining with all his strength to hold them out about a foot apart straight in front of him, Himmelhoch began to speak for the first time in complete sentences and paragraphs in a colloquial though heavily accented

English. These were specialized divining rods, the holy man instructed, specifically endowed with the power to pick up auras from the energy field of the dead. Gilguli must stretch out the rods, exactly as shown, and ask them the question, Are there dead in this ground? When the rods crossed, the answer was yes. Then he must remember to say, Thank you, rods, and repeat the operation. He must speak to the rods nicely, Himmelhoch cautioned, never lash out or strike with them, and in this way, if in no other, he would surpass—no comparison intended, God forbid—even Moses our teacher who transgressed with his staff by smiting the rock. Even as Himmelhoch was explaining, the rods were crossing furiously under their own power, no matter how strenuously the holy man struggled to keep them apart, clanking together again and again as they picked up the frequencies and vibrations emanating from the dead in every direction. This, of course, was not surprising, as the two men were wielding the rods in the neighborhood of the ancient cemetery descending along the slope of the Mount of Olives, which overflowed with the righteous departed awaiting resurrection, longing through eternity for the blast of the shofar that would signal the final roll down the hill to the Golden Gate cast wide open at last and onto the restored Temple Mount toward blissful redemption. Himmelhoch passed the rods to Gilguli and gave him the assignment to go forth and practice his technique until the next morning, when he must return to his master to recount all that he had learned.

What he had learned, Gilguli reported the next day, was that, although admittedly out of shape as befitted his new incarnation as a Jew, not even with all the upper-body strength he had acquired from years of crew and wrestling and lacrosse in his renounced life at prep school and Princeton could he keep the rods from crossing like crazy—every step he took, no matter where he walked, notwithstanding all of his exertions, the rods crossed. He could do nothing to stop them. Himmelhoch nodded his head mournfully; the boy had done his homework at least. This phenomenon was to be expected, the holy man elucidated, due to the fact that the entire country, from Metula to Eilat, from the river Jordan to the Mediterranean Sea, was a graveyard. Since time immemorial people have come here to die, Himmelhoch went on, and that includes those who come with the conscious intention of dying as well as those who come with the illusion that they might live, while the rest have their remains shipped in pine boxes in the bellies of the great jets. Israel, as everyone must have heard by now, is a land that devours its inhabitants. Then Himmelhoch commanded Gilguli to take the rods and set out for Poland. There he would find the ashes of Yankel Galitzianer. That is where he would find himself.

It was late July when Jacob Gilguli landed in Warsaw. With his knapsack on his back and the two metal rods erect and quivering before him, he embarked by foot on a pilgrimage to the death camps, fasting all day until sunset and concentrating his brain waves on the mantras of the Jewish prayers, Shema Yisrael, Kaddish, Dayenu, a few others, which he had memorized on the Sabbath in the meditation hall of a charismatic shepherd who gathered his flock of lost souls at the Western Wall. He headed first in the direction of Treblinka, where, according to the *Never Again* guidebook he carried in his fanny pack along with his passport and credit cards and zlotys, over three quarters of a million Jews were exterminated. Of course the rods went berserk when he arrived there, but it was also the case, he could not deny it, that however hard he tried to restrain them they kept on crossing, they had a will of their own, they crossed almost every step of the way, on every superficially neutral road and highway he traversed, though when he set foot on the killing grounds he believed there was a difference in degree—there they went into an absolute off-the-charts frenzy of crossing, he believed. Still, how might Himmelhoch in the enlightenment of his cave have interpreted this riddle of chronic rod activity even in the lands of the gentiles? The holy man, Gilguli told himself, would have taught that tragedy and atrocity, suffering and death are fermenting just below the surface everywhere, leaving no trace, offering no meaning, wherever there was once life—and gentiles, too, may be considered a life form, Himmelhoch might have glossed, also God's creatures whether we like it or not, never mind if they saw fit to classify Jews as subhuman, Jewish blood as racially inferior, Jewish life as unworthy of life. Hadn't the Master of the Universe sent his own prophet Jonah to save the more than 120,000 idolaters of Nineveh who could not tell their right from their left, not to mention all of the animals?

Gilguli proceeded southward with rods pointing valiantly in the direction of Sobibor (a quarter million gassed, cf. *Never Again*, including, it must be conceded, some non-Jews with mothers). Streams of gleaming buses with banners—Holocaust Experience, Heritage Mission, Back to the Source, The Nation of Israel Lives, We Are Here!—passed him by, conveying tourists he recognized as Jews not only by features and costume and loud complaints about the air-conditioning, which he could make out through the opening windows, but also, to his mortification, by the inevitable gesture of pausing mid-greeting, freezing mid-wave, and then the shouts, "Hey, wait a minute—that guy's not Jewish, it's some kind of hippie or something—Hey pal, what's with the sticks?" Only the German youth groups on their required mass guilt trip in a bus labeled Roots Kanal, the straps of their lederhosen and the feathers of their Tyrolean hats visible through the panes, howling, "Ja, ja, ja, ja," at the tops of their lungs, hailed him warmly and fraternally as they hurtled obediently onward to do the next death camp. At the entrance to Majdanek (215,000 from starvation, torture, and disease; 145,000 by gassing or shooting—were the words "numbers" and "numbing" derived from the same root, Gilguli wondered), he was stopped by the dark-skinned, gold-chained Israeli proprietor of a kiosk selling death camp T-shirts and postcards, Holocaust trinkets and knick-knacks, who drew out from a secret compartment under his table a pile of authentic artifacts and memorabilia—"Only for our most discriminating customers," he confided—and hustled Gilguli into buying a yellow badge with the word "Juif" imprinted on it to attach to the other side of his skullcap—"So that they'll recognize you from the front *and* the rear." Even as Gilguli demurred, another product was flashed, a one hundred percent genuine knockoff, much cheaper, a yellow star stamped with the word "Jew" for an English-speaking market. And that was when, with the peddler hissing in disgust after him that he could go around with a sack on his head decorated all over with yellow stars like some kind of wizard, he'd still never pass—"And by the way, *haver*, what's with the sticks?"—that was when Gilguli realized that if he was ever to connect with the remains of his former life he needed to get off the beaten track, he needed to ask the rods the correct question, he needed a sign.

The first sign came in the form of *Never Again* opening of itself to the words "out of the way," "practically in Ukraine," "end of the earth," "neglected," "forgotten"—"God forsaken." Jacob Gilguli surrendered to the sign, setting out to the southeast as if pulled down by ropes. That was how he arrived on a bright morning toward the end of summer at what he hoped might be his final destination, as the airline pilots like to say: the Belzec death camp in the far depths of Poland, where, consulting *Never Again*, from March to December of 1942, 600,000 Jews mostly from southern Poland, including quite plausibly his former self when he was Yankel Galitzianer of Przemysl, were offloaded from cattle cars, gassed with carbon monoxide, dumped into great pits, then dug up again, haphazardly cremated, and reburied in the rush to blot out the evidence. Gilguli lowered his eyes and took off his shoes before treading upon camp ground. He stepped onto the gray ash that stretched endlessly before him like the remnants of a cosmic bonfire; a hard white substance was strewn everywhere, reminding him of sea shells, cutting into the soles of his feet. "Will these bones live?" Gilguli spoke out loud. That was the question for the rods, and it burst from his throat on its own, the way an animal squeal leaps spontaneously from a person who recalls something shameful. It was as if he had been seized by the shock of prophetic madness. Raising his eyes from the ash-and-bone-blanketed soil, he was rewarded at once with the second sign.

Figures in the foreground with metal rods outstretched were roaming the devastated landscape, multiple shapes like his own almost floating in the early morning light, divining for the dead. How could Jacob Gilguli doubt for one moment that this astonishing replication of his own mission, men everywhere dowsing for corpses, was the definitive sign he had been praying for? This was what he took in at once, his image mirrored, as a man's gaze originating from deep within his consciousness and obsessions will settle first upon his own reflection and only then turn to take in what surrounds it. Only then did he see the mounds of freshly excavated earth rising everywhere, swirling into focus, the upheaval of a construction site—he saw a bulldozer, a cement mixer, a crane, earth-moving trucks, and farther back, the green cubicle of a portable toilet. Struggling like the other seekers to hold out his rods against the overwhelming crossing force rising from the stirred-up dead, Gilguli made his way deeper into the camp, a dog at his heels leaping exuberantly to sniff at his warm parts. Would it be sacrilege, he wondered, to use one of these rods to get rid of the dog? Here and there he noticed men sitting on camp stools with buckets at their sides, bandanas wrapped around their heads to sop up the percolating heat of this late summer's day, jiving on their perches to the beat from their headphones, pushing down between their spread legs on drills probing deep into the earth. From one of these drillers, a Polish kid transmitting in video English, the cigarette in the corner of his mouth bobbing dryly, spilling ashes to ashes, Gilguli learned that what they were doing here—the rod wielders, the drillers, and so on—was knocking themselves out to pinpoint the locations of the remains, the bodies, the corpses, the mass graves, the burial pits, yadayada, in order to cover their rears against charges of plowing through the dead in the process of creating a memorial in their honor. The memorial was slated to be a narrow pathway cutting through the entire camp, starting at ground level, then slowly, slowly descending to, say, ten meters deep before dead-ending at a wall—Very major chills and thrills for the visitor walking this walk, the driller said, goose pimples big-time, you feel like trapped, suffocation, buried alive, can't breathe, get me out of here, but after you've done the tour, you feel good, you feel very, very good, you go into town, you look for something to eat, something to buy, go on, treat yourself, do something nice for yourself, you deserve it, you are on the side of the good.

Gilguli was shaking with emotion. He felt himself almost physically overcome by the noble concept underlying this memorial—of vicarious suffering, of sympathetic dying, of entering this constricting passageway, penetrating the space of the dead, the victims pressing in against you from both sides with flattened palms and frozen screams, he could almost see them as through the glass walls of a fish tank, and yes, feeling their pain, experiencing what it must have been like to be them. It took everything in Gilguli's power to refrain from lowering himself then and there into the ash-and-bone-laced depths that had been exposed even at that stage of the digging in order to achieve the blessed state of becoming one with the dead. What could this uneducated Polish kid from this anus mira-bilis of the world possibly understand about aesthetics? This was not your usual kitsch, it was not schlock, it was a shattering memorial concept, a brilliant design, moving beyond words— if this didn't force you to feel something, nothing ever would, you were a lost cause. Problem is, the kid was now saying, the dead are everywhere, you can't dig this ditch without smashing into them, shaking them up—above ground, below ground, it's bodies all over the place, bodies all the way down. He gestured at the contents of one of the buckets beside him. Gilguli noted a portion of a skull sprouting a tuft of hair cushioned in ash, a piece of femur on a bed of bone fragments. The kid drew his drill out of the ground and indicated a chunk of waxy black stuff in its scoop. "Fat," he said, and plopped it into a bucket.

Coming toward them now was a delegation of four men in suits and ties, all wrestling with the rods. From a distance they appeared almost identical: short, squat, bald, the three older ones with cardboard yarmulkes peaking on top of their heads, the younger, slightly taller one with a glossy black beard clearly set apart, the leader, the guide, sporting on his head a well-worn crocheted model with the phrase "Belzec, My Little Village, Belzec" worked into the rim—Rabbi Heshie Lemberger, American-born from Brooklyn, New York, the driller informed Gilguli, as Virgil is said to have informed Dante, recently condemned to be chief rabbi of greater Poland with a congregation of more or less three thousand souls above ground, moonlighting here as fundraiser for the Belzec memorial project, giving the grand tour to prospective donors, those three little fat guys with the tepees on their heads, survivors of the Holocaust from southern Poland, Galicia, morphed into real estate titans from Florida, Miami.

Translating this as the third sign, Gilguli instantly attached himself to this contingent, sticking fast even in the face of unconcealed irritation from the three little moguls—they didn't even bother to lower their voices when inquiring of each other in chopped-liver accents, "Who let in this guy, did he bought a ticket or what, didn't they told us it was a private red-carpet tour what we was getting?" Still, Gilguli hung on relentlessly, tagging along behind as the rabbi patiently instructed them in correct rod technique—"Do sticks like this, boys"—demonstrating how and vigorously asserting that, cutting-edge scientific advances notwithstanding, nothing, not even all the systematic drilling along a mathematical grid and so forth and so on, has yet proved as effective as two simple divination rods in finding the dead. "This is not mumbo jumbo, friends, it is not hocus pocus or black magic or voodoo or witchcraft or idolatry, God forbid, *avodah zarah*, no way—this is an ancient method, the wisdom of the ages, tried and true like chicken soup, like pearls from the lips of your *bubbes* and *zeydes*, may they rest in peace." His gaze took in the desolation of the old folks' resting place surrounding him, the churned-up topography of where they lay beneath his feet.

Turning sharply, the rabbi marched his troops, with Gilguli bringing up the rear, to a forlorn tree standing apart and wrapped both arms around it in a rapturous embrace. "You see this tree, my friends?" the rabbi cried. "This tree was here during the killings. The younger trees we chop down, naturally, to make room for the memorial, but this one is holy, this one we let stand. Why? Because it bore witness. So we call it a Witness Tree. It's a very great mitzvah to sustain such a sacred tree—he who performs a good deed of this magnitude will not only earn a place in the world to come, munching on leviathan and wild ox, sipping honey mead and enjoying the luxury of having his wife as his personal footstool, but he will also be privileged in this life to have the tree named in his honor, with a beautiful engraved plaque in solid brass affixed to it so attesting." Reflexively, the three donors began to grope inside their jackets for their checkbooks. "Relax, friends, it's all right, you can pay on the way out, we trust you completely. And even if you happen to forget, don't worry, it's okay—we'll just lock you in here for the night until you send us the check, that's all—ha ha, just kidding, just kidding."

With an indulgent laugh, the rabbi then went on to reassure his three willing contributors that in addition to the witness trees there were plenty of other ways they could support the Belzec memorial project; for example, by endowing a position in one of their names, like a chair at a university, for an assistant who could fill in for him in supervising the memorial construction on site when he was called away by his pastoral duties elsewhere in greater Poland or was obliged to travel abroad for fundraising or other purposes, as was so often the case. He already had someone in mind for this assistant job, as it happened, but unfortunately he had not yet been able to raise the necessary funds, however modest, to cover the stipend—"Not some fancy expert or anything, this fellow I'm thinking about, not a scholar in Jewish law and ritual pertaining to the handling of the dead and so on, no big genius, but between you and me, businessman to businessman, exactly right for our purposes—a warm body, a fact on the ground we can put in place and point to when the protesters and fanatics out there, the destroyers, my friends, not the builders like you, start up again like clockwork with their yelling and hollering: Desecration of the Dead, Violation of Victims' Remains, and so on and so forth. With God's help and yours, friends, I've found just the right man for the job, and believe me, it wasn't so easy, not too many normal human beings would be willing to work in a place like this, a haunted house, a ghost town, a hell hole, a terrible place, of course, terrible, terrible—we should never forget for one minute, it goes without saying." Then, sweeping his arm in the direction of Jacob Gilguli, the rabbi requested him to step forward and introduce himself. The three donors turned in unison, their necks craning audibly, to bestow an appraising look on the face hovering like a strange fruit more than a foot above them. Gilguli nodded formally to the rabbi, like a junior partner acknowledging his boss before starting a presentation, and crossed his metal rods ceremoniously in front of his chest. "Yankel Galitzianer," Gilguli said, "the rabbi's assistant"—and a moment later, had the satisfaction, albeit not unalloyed, of hearing one of his new patrons remark, "Go on, a Galitzianer no less. And the whole time I'm thinking he's just some dumb goy. Who would believe? Live and learn!"

And so Jacob Gilguli dedicated himself to the dead. He took a room in the nearby town of Belzec, in the home of a widow called Kaczka. He never learned if this was her given name or her family name; in accordance with the proper manner in which he had been brought up to address an older person of the female persuasion, he respectfully called her Ma'am, including in bed. It was at the Belzec railway station, the terminus that had, after all, made the transports to the death camp so convenient and efficient, that the ancient dispatcher directed him to Kaczka's for lodging, an ideal match for this American, as the widow was famous locally for her mastery of the English language, having spent much of her adult life in Chicago, where she and her husband, the late Bolek, had operated a Polish deli. After Bolek's passing, fortified by his life insurance policy and a monthly social security check, she signed over the business to her son, Bolek the younger, and made her way back to end her days where they had begun, in her childhood village of Belzec, where she supplemented her income with boarders in the house and chickens and pigs in the yard. That was where Gilguli saw her for the first time—in the yard, mucking out the chicken coops in a flowered housecoat and rubber galoshes, her broad, ruddy, babushka-framed face reminding him at once of the Polish pope—the same sturdy peasant stock. She turned to him, as he approached with his knapsack on his back and his rods in his hands, as if she had been expecting him all along, and shook her head sadly, pointing to the worn-out, bedraggled hens. "That old cock he is killing them for sure, he don't leave them in peace for one minute even," she said. Those were her first words to him, delivered in a Slavic-accented no-frills mid-western American. A feminist for my sins, Gilguli thought; his instinct was they could do business.

Every morning, with Kaczka's blessings, he mounted the ancient bicycle that he found leaning in her shed, and with his rods tied to his back like arrows in the quiver of a hunt-er-gatherer, and the shofar that he had purchased from Abu Shahid cradled in the shredded wicker basket tied to the handlebars, he pedaled off to the death camp. His responsi-bilities were twofold, as the rabbi had outlined them that first day while the three donors sat in the limousine and refreshed themselves with slivovitz poured by the Polish driver. Number one, first and foremost, he must be vigilantly on guard against the protesters, our own people unfortunately, the rabbi was sorry to say, who could descend on them unannounced, at any moment, like biological warfare so to speak, with their self-righteous accusations of desecration of the dead, blah-blah-blah, occupying the site, planting their bodies in the path of the construction, sabotaging the works, creating a hullabaloo and ruckus and scandal that would reek far and wide—obviously not a good thing for the Jews, not to mention the repercussions for their financial investment in this memorial, already considerable, already well into the millions. To deal with this very real threat, the rabbi armed Gilguli with a cell phone and specific instructions to immediately alert not only him, wherever in the world he might happen to be, but above all the relevant Polish officials who were equipped to move in fast in the event of a raid by the Jewish lunatics and take the necessary action, the less said on this subject the better; in such a case, the rabbi decreed with the full weight of the divine authority vested in him, it was not only permissible to remain a silent bystander while the storm troopers did what they had to do, it was actually a mitzvah. Gilguli's second task, the rabbi went on, was to keep his eyes peeled for human remains, but in that department, the rabbi cautioned him, he must use his common sense, he must be extremely careful not to insult the Polish workers, who could become very touchy and sensitive as a result of the slightest critical innuendo. If, for example, he happened to notice body parts being dumped out with the garbage or crushed under the wheels of a truck or soiled by the foreman's dog Bogdan, the thing to do was to quietly and discreetly gather them up on a piece of newspaper or something, dispose of them in one of the officially marked burial mounds, and maybe whisper a little prayer if he happened to know one by heart, but by all means do not make a big show of it, please. Beyond that, visitors should be kept strictly off the premises during the construction phase due to the attendant hazards, and this includes not only the idly curious, but also relatives of the victims who might show up on pilgrimages to pay their respects, no matter what distances they have traveled to this blighted corner of the planet; however much they may beg and cajole, politely but firmly he must bar them from approaching or viewing the operation in progress, the way a patient is prevented, for his own good, in the interest of ultimate healing, of sparing him unnecessary psychological trauma, from seeing his own entrails exposed and the organs or tissues, solid or liquid, being extracted from his insides during a surgical procedure. At the end of each day's shift, when dark descended upon the death camp and all the workers went home, the rabbi expected to receive a full report by email—a duty that Gilguli took pains to execute every evening from a rundown little internet café in the heart of the town of Belzec, where the screen saver showed a collage of multiple, identical stooped figures with hooked noses and lascivious lips and rubbing hands clutching money bags, who, he had to admit, really did not resemble him at all. The rabbi looked up into Gilguli's blue-blooded eyes in an effort to probe the level of comprehension of this alien creature. "So, have we covered all the ground?" he asked with an awkward laugh, gesturing in spite of himself at the expanse of the death camp stretching behind them. Without waiting for an answer, the rabbi clapped his new assistant on the bicep and swiveled abruptly to join his donors in the waiting limousine, its engine already growling. That was the last time Gilguli saw him, except for one other occasion, in a large appliance store some years later, when the rabbi showed up on the screens of several dozen television sets, one of three experts on a panel offering insights on the topic "Holocausts—Yours, Mine, Ours." The rabbi had put on considerable weight, even from his talking heads that was manifest, and had shaved off his beard; nevertheless, Gilguli fingered him in the lineup again and again, no problem, he was not fooled for a minute.

From the internet café, he made his way each evening back to Kaczka's, where a hot supper awaited him: potato soup with black bread, kasha and mushrooms, vodka and tea. He had declared himself a vegetarian that first day when he followed her into her kitchen and saw the knives and cleavers and the empty casings hanging like an old lady's stockings and the great tubs of blood on the table and the butcher boards heaped with the chopped-up fat and intestines to stuff the winter sausages. Kaczka only laughed and observed that she had heard somewhere that Hitler was a vegetarian too, but hey, you're the customer, mister. As the nights grew longer and colder, as the savage onset of their unacknowledged gropings glided into a kind of comfortable comradeship, they would lie side by side beneath the great mound of the goose-down quilt and talk quietly, sometimes until the rooster took a break and dismounted from the hens to give out a crow. Gilguli opened his heart to her, told her everything, poured out all his sufferings and humiliations and doubts, held nothing back—emptying himself in the dark without shame, without fear of consequences, into this old woman who did not matter, after all, who was invisible even in daylight and would soon disappear altogether from this cursed and barren edge of the universe, taking his secrets with her to eternal cold storage. He told her about his past lives and his present, about his days standing watch against the protesters, the self-proclaimed Jewish guardians of the dead, the extremists and obstructionists, who could swoop down any minute without warning and park themselves with their white prayer shawls hooded over their heads, clogging up the memorial works. He told her about the Polish diggers tunneling out the underground walkway, tossing ash and bone over the sides, stuffing a hunk of jawbone in a pocket to bring to a girlfriend for a souvenir. Passionately he strove to explain to her how pierced to the very core he was by the idea of communing with the dead through descent into the depths of this memorial pathway; this was not a ghoulish concept, it was not sick, this was as close to the real thing as one who had not been privileged to be there in this life could get, it was almost too much to take in—all he wanted was to go down and curl up in that crevice forever, sex was nothing in comparison, this was a full-body-penetration experience, the birth canal transformed into death canal. Gilguli could feel Kaczka nodding her approval in the darkness beside him. "Like the tube," she said—which, she told him, was what they called the narrow path the naked Jews were herded through in the death camp, between the undressing room and the gas chamber. When she was a small girl during the war, she used to play tube with her little friends. It was their second favorite game, after doctor. "Yes, just like the tube," Kaczka said—and therefore, for Belzec, a very appropriate memorial idea.

She could see the construction equipment from a distance, she said, the cranes especially. It looked from a distance like a very major project, very impressive, but personally she'd rather not get too close, she did not like to go into the camp anymore, she was too old for that now, though the truth is, for years after the war, when the Communists took over from the Nazis, all the kids used to sneak out there at night—what else was there for a young person with hormones to do in this miserable place? We would make bonfires there, roast chunks of meat on sticks, drink beer, dance to the transistor radio, make out—necking and petting, like they used to say in the States, until they skipped over that stage for good—go all the way. Yes, she too, she had to confess. It was so creepy, so sexy, and our parents could never find us, they would never dare go into the camp at night, guaranteed. It was just lay back and enjoy. But even if she personally at this stage in her life had outgrown the camp, she was glad to see the cranes in there, glad about this memorial project, Kaczka said. Of course, she could not predict what the local hooligans might take it into their heads to do to the memorial once it was completed, they were already pretty pissed at the Jews for everything that happened to them, and frankly, she couldn't imagine who in his right mind would be willing to trek all the way out to this bunghole of the world just to take a stroll through one morbid crack in the ground and hit a stone wall—but who knows? Maybe a death camp is a great natural resource after all, maybe the memorial will be good for the town, bring down the tourists and sightseers and shoppers and eaters, maybe business will finally go boom. The cranes in there now, to build this memorial, Kaczka told Gilguli, reminded her of the ones she used to see during the war, when she was still a small girl—you know how children everywhere are so interested in giant machines, girls too for your information, for some reason they find this fascinating, like dragons, like dinosaurs, her grandchildren are crazy about them also, Kaczka said with a fond laugh. Yes, during the war, before they finally left for good, the Germans also brought cranes into the camp, she told Gilguli, to lift the dead bodies out of the burial pits. At first, they used Jewish prisoners for this filthy job, to dig up the bodies and cremate them, but then with all the pressure to finish up and get out fast, they brought in the heavy machinery, they brought in the cranes. They would lift the rotting corpses out of the pits with these cranes, the Germans, and roast them on great bonfires. She could see the flames leaping up night after night when she was a small girl during the war, the black smoke rising. Some of the bodies were so swollen and decayed they had turned into liquid, that's what her father told her, like a Black Forest fairy tale—imagine telling such horror stories to an innocent child, a baby almost, but, hey, this was in the time before mental health. The smell for miles around was unbearable. We all walked around like outlaws in the cowboy movies in those days, with handkerchiefs tied across our faces because of the terrible stink when the Germans were burning the corpses, just before they left town for good. Everyone blamed the Jews for polluting the air.

Then, as soon as those lousy Germans were gone, Kaczka told Gilguli, the whole town descended on the death camp to search for treasure. It was like a public holiday—schools closed, people took off from work, everyone felt justified, we had a right, we deserved it, nothing could stop us, not even the swarms of flies that formed a black canopy over our heads, this was our reparations for how we had been humiliated, for all we had suffered. And what we found among the remains of the dead was beyond imagining, unbelievable what the Jews had managed to bring along with them in the cattle cars, my own father invested in a metal detector to poke for valuables among the ashes and the bones and the fat and the half-burned corpses in the burial pits. There were pots and pans, cutlery, dentures, luggage, artificial limbs, musical instruments, tools, even some sewing machines, furniture, picture frames, eyeglasses, pocketknives and pens, toiletry articles, sports equipment for recreation, including skis and, believe it or not, a bicycle, and also silver and gold, not to mention the hundreds of gold teeth that the corpse-dentists had missed, and coins from all over the world, and jewelry, jewelry, jewelry; when she was living in America during the seventies and eighties, Kaczka said, there used to be signs in front of all the synagogues, Save Soviet Jewelry, Jews are very big on jewelry in case you haven't noticed. And the gems we found in the death camp, it was like the road to paradise, a fortune in stones: diamonds, emeralds, sapphires, rubies, pearls buried in the ashes, they must have been hidden inside the bodies in unmentionable places, even the Germans with all their efficiency missed more than you could ever dream of during their inspections of the private parts of the corpses, but they had a point after all, those lousy Germans, they weren't imagining things, the Jews were walking treasure chests—it took the fires of cremation to get them to give up their jewels once and for all.

It was still wartime when this happened, Kaczka told Gilguli, and you can imagine how embarrassing it was for the Germans—after all the trouble they'd gone to, getting rid of the incriminating evidence and all—when they got wind of how we were swarming all over the place, picking it clean. So one day they closed off the death camp—just like that, they closed it off, declared it off limits. They stuck in some trees and bushes to give it a nice peaceful look and handed it over as a present to one of their Ukrainian guards to farm with his family. That was the last straw, the final insult, handing over Polish soil to a Ukrainian—primitives, barbarians, animals, every last one of them, not a single one of them is any damn good. The Germans, at least, are a cultured nation, civilized; at night after a hard day's work they would sit down like members of the human race to listen to classical music played by the orchestra of Jewish prisoners, Schubert, Beethoven, sometimes we could hear it too, when it wasn't being drowned out by one of their drunken orgies—but hey, who could begrudge them a little relaxation? They were a long way from home after all, they missed their mamas and their pretty little Schatzis and their little doggie Putzi, all day long they were killing themselves processing Jews with only Ukrainians for company—whipping, beating, torturing, shooting, unloading the cattle cars, and sending the cargo straight from the undressing rooms through the tube into the gas chambers, and after the gassing, there was the nasty business of removing the bodies to make room for the next load, it wasn't so easy dragging those Jews out of the gas chambers, that's what everyone said, they were frozen solid, whole families were stuck together, you could tell them apart, even in death they were still holding hands.

Kaczka reached over in the darkness and took Gilguli's hand, gliding her fingers up to the tender underside of his forearm where his number was tattooed and tracing it familiarly. "No way you got this in Belzec in your past life, darling," Kaczka said. "In Belzec, it was straight off the cattle cars and into the gas chambers. In Belzec, the Ukrainians and Germans didn't fool around. In Belzec, it was one hundred percent anonymous, one hundred percent assembly line, one hundred percent death factory. No tattoo for you in Belzec, mister—sorry. If you're looking for tattoos, try Auschwitz, that's my recommendation. Yes, in Belzec it was trains all the time, trains coming in through the night, twenty, forty, sixty cars long, engines screeching in the dark, dogs and Ukrainians barking, Germans shouting, Jews wailing. No one could ever get any sleep. Everyone blamed the Jews for keeping them up all night long."

He woke in the night with his heart pounding, because of the screams. The protesters were there, he realized this at once. Fumbling in the dark for his cell phone, he could only put his hands on his rods and the ram's horn. He staggered out into the yard with nothing more than a sheet wrapped around his body. In her black rubber galoshes, illuminated by the headlights of her old pickup truck, Kaczka was plunging a knife into the heart of a pig. The pig was trussed up with ropes, screaming human screams—desperate, terrified shrieks. Gilguli began to run, first toward the train station, and from there, half a kilometer farther to the point of the railway spur inside the death camp where the cattle cars were unloaded. Yes, the protesters had come out, it was just as he had thought, they had appeared at last, he had been waiting so long, he had expected them sooner. They had congregated in the night—it was guerrilla theater cunningly plotted, ruthlessly staged, hundreds of thousands of protesters in diaphanous white shrouds, refracting their own cold light, their faces hollow and unforgiving, emitting a low hum that thickened the air, filling every space of the death camp to its distant edge. The rods in Gilguli's hands were shaking uncontrollably. They fell to the ground and slithered away. He followed behind them, cutting through the massed protesters as if they were cobwebs, clouds, smoke, into the invading fissure that had stirred them up on this night. The protesters were closing in on him, he could feel them behind him along the entire length of his body, like the shades and spirits that had pursued him down the long dark hallways of his childhood. Without daring to turn around, he fled into the excavation, slid down the slope of the ravaged grave, into the heart of the disturbance in the field, down to its lowest depths. There he crouched down, naked among the snakes and the scorpions, huddling against the cold, his hands clamped against his ears. The protesters were bearing in on him from all sides, letting out their otherworldly hum that penetrated his head without passing through his ears, raging, raging, demanding the final sustained blast of the shofar that would bring down the heavens on all their tormentors.

Dead Zone

The case is now closed on the reasons behind the decision by the United Nations to officially terminate the existence of Israel as a living entity, an event that occurred about a century after it had voted for the partition of the Holy Land leading to the establishment of the Jewish State in 1948. But when the dissolution took place—and though I was still only a child at the time, I remember it acutely mainly because of the peculiar relevance it possessed to my family history—the discussions and arguments were ferocious, blacking out all other news for an attention span notably longer than is customarily allotted to even the most seminal time-line events.

Now, though, nobody talks about it anymore. Those who opposed the decision, mostly Jews naturally (but also some fundamentalist Christian fellow travelers outraged that they'd lost their shot at rapture), have added the day of the UN declaration ending Israel to the Jewish calendar along with all the other catastrophic dates set aside for mourning and fasting and other forms of self-mortification. The majority of more moderate representatives of the human race, however, have absorbed the fact on the ground and moved on, and the reasons for why it happened have been filed away in the category of common knowledge, generally accepted conventional wisdom: First, that Israel had already been mostly emptied out and sucked dry by then anyway, brain-drained, the best and the brightest, and, many maintained, also the most ethical Jews having long ago packed their bags and left the country in disgust and despair, seeking opportunities and meaning elsewhere on the planet. Second, Jews as a type, it has historically been proved, contribute more and conduct themselves with far greater moral rigor and a far more urgent sense of their role-model responsibilities as the Chosen People when operating as a diaspora curiosity. And finally, it was actually in the interest of living Jews not to be clumped together on one plot of earth in the God-forsaken Middle East or anywhere else, conveniently in-gathered in the so-called Promised Land, a concentrated sitting-duck target awaiting inevitable annihilation in a nuclear blast that would eliminate them from the system in a single flash. In short, the UN resolution to abolish Israel was fundamentally good for the Jews. This was the accepted dogma as packaged in the media, and taught in schools and in universities as well. It's what I learned and believed too.

It's entirely possible, of course, that in the future some ambitious young revisionist historians will emerge burning to make names for themselves by gutting the discourse, arguing, for example, that the action taken by the UN was just another manifestation of anti-Semitism masquerading as anti-Zionism, or that it happened because the world was sick of forever rewarding the Jews for their tiresome Holocaust, or that it was part of a secret deal with the Muslim states to calm them down by extracting this alien growth called Israel from their midst (if so, the evidence shows it didn't work). On one point, though, everyone was in agreement at the time, when the UN took this radical step, and remains so to this day, and for myself I can't envision this consensus ever changing at any point in the future. There is not a soul who does not agree that the final solution to the Israel question that the United Nations came up with was stunningly brilliant, strikingly elegant in its simplicity and even in its obviousness, like a mathematics or physics problem that had vexed humankind for millennia, that some young genius suddenly solves one bright day with a single-line equation of absolute purity and clarity, undeniable truth.

How that august body so ingeniously eliminated Israel as a state was simply by designating it a UNESCO World Heritage Site—specifically, as the world's largest Jewish cemetery. There was no question that Israel fulfilled the World Heritage criteria in that it possessed outstanding universal value and bore testimony to a great and unique cultural tradition and civilization, living or dead. Above all, by being granted this status, Israel, even as a dedicated massive graveyard populated exclusively by the dead, was legally protected by the Laws of War as defined in the Geneva Convention from all military and hostile acts that might be directed against it.

The way this translated in practical terms was that all those still living in Israel when the resolution came down—the majority of them leftover Jews but also non-Jews, mainly Christians and Muslims—were compelled to leave the country, giving it over to its rightful owners, the Jewish dead, who already outnumbered the living by vast multitudes. No doubt about it—Israel was already basically a necropolis, like the rose-stoned city of

Petra, from the north to the south, east to west, from Metula to Eilat, from the Dead Sea to the Mediterranean. Even for Jews still living in the most remote spots on earth, in places in which you'd never expect to find anyone who looks Jewish, even for such Jews Israel remained the most desirable place in which to spend eternity. As my father used to say whenever we passed a cemetery (usually in New Jersey), "Everyone is dying to get in there." This joke can be applied to Israel in spades.

Now, under the UN declaration, only Jews could be buried in Israel. Those of other faiths already underground there were grandfathered in, allowed to remain undisturbed, their cemeteries closed for business and walled off. As for living persons, there were here as everywhere on this earth the forgotten and expendable, useless and unwanted, squatters who had hidden in their holes and hung on, burrowing and scavenging, but they were few in number and of no account, motherless children who soon would become extinct as civilization evolved. The only ones granted residence in Israel, and solely on a temporary basis, were rotating crews of caretakers of the Jewish cemeteries and burial grounds, and the officials, religious and secular, charged with ministering to them and guarding them; for shorter periods, the builders of new facilities to accommodate the nonstop shipments of Jewish corpses from the four corners of the globe to the Holy Land to await the trumpet blast of the messiah that would awaken the dead; and for even briefer and more highly controlled periods (a few days at most), the living bearing their dead for interment or arriving for the unveiling of a monument over a gravesite (though with time, this became less and less necessary, as such rituals could be carried out by the officials on site while the survivors watched from abroad via live streaming), or relatives making a pilgrimage to pay homage to an ancestor or loved one, and to set down a stone marking their visit.

There have been many gasbags who have poked their heads out of their holes to take credit for this brilliant solution to the Israel problem. This is not something I want to go into, as frankly, it makes me crazy—I feel it as a personal assault on my family's honor. After all, the World Heritage status accorded with the full authority of the United Nations, along with all the benefits and protections that came with it, hung on the realization that Israel was in fact already a cemetery all the way down. And where did that idea come from? Not from the Bible, not from the book of Genesis, as some claim, in the chapter on the circumcision covenant, when in exchange for generations of Jewish foreskins God promised, among other goodies, to give the land to Abraham and to his descendants as an *Akhuzat Olam*, an eternal holding, which can only mean a cemetery ("*beit olam*" in Hebrew, in Aramaic, "*beit almin*"). For only the domain of death is possessed everlastingly.

No. Whether the public realizes this or not, the idea that Israel already housed wall-to-wall dead was planted in the consciousness of the human race by the extraordinary events surrounding the burial of my great-grandfather Isadore "Izzy" Gam, which took place about ten years before the UNESCO designation of Israel as the world's largest Jewish cemetery. My great-grandfather's funeral was also carried in the news, almost with the same focus and intensity as the World Heritage announcement itself. As far as I am concerned, there's no doubt that Great-Grandpa Izzy's burial saga was the seed that sprouted into the World Heritage designation that in the end saved Israel for the Jews, albeit only for the dead ones, which every Jew (in this respect no different from any other mortal) would in any event sooner or later become, one way or another. You can say that my great-grandfather Izzy Gam was the Theodor Herzl of Jewish continuity and permanence in Zion, Herzl gone to the dark side by force of necessity and circumstances, which is why I feel compelled to come forward now to remind the world of his remarkable contribution, in order that he might finally be honored with the recognition that is rightfully his due.

I was only three years old when my great-grandfather Izzy Gam died in the year 2040, at a good old age, eighty-seven, despite all the physical suffering he had endured in his life. This means that I was certainly too young at the time to remember firsthand the incredible odyssey that distinguished his burial, which transfixed the world and became not only a major news story, a full account of which is available on the record for any member of the general public interested in checking the facts, but also an integral part of our family legacy. Yet despite the insistence by most experts that human beings retain no memories of events that occur prior to the age of five, I have two very stark recollections related to my great-grandfather Izzy. The first had to do with his size. It seemed to me then that he was about my height, the height of a three-year-old, or at most just a bit taller, a suitable playmate. Admittedly, this may not be a true memory, it may be a detail I subsequently learned about him or something garnered from photographs I saw. But the second is without doubt an authentic memory, and has to do with his funeral, which, despite my extreme youth, I was required to participate in as a significant member of the immediate family—at that time, the only male great-grandchild.

It took place in New York, at the Fifth Avenue Synagogue, and was attended by thousands, both inside the sanctuary and massed outside, due to the fact that his late wife, my great-grandmother Judi, was the only child of the sensationally wealthy real estate magnate and Holocaust survivor Sigi Weiner. Although she was several years younger than Great-Grandpa Izzy, Great-Grandma Judi was struck down early by that Ashkenazi specialty—like gefilte fish—breast cancer. Even her father's dazzling fortune could not save her. But testimony to the family's enormous wealth as it touched upon the passing of my great-grandfather Izzy can be found in the impressive number of paid obituary notices that appeared in the *New York Times* for an entire week following his death, placed by organizations and individuals who had been beneficiaries of the Weiner largesse and hoped to remain on the receiving end in the future. All of this I don't remember firsthand, naturally. I know it from family lore, and also from my own research into the subject.

What I do remember, however, and very keenly, is something that took place after the funeral itself, and the ride in a cortège of limousines to Kennedy Airport: Great-Grandpa Izzy's coffin being raised into the air by a yellow forklift truck at the El Al cargo depot in anticipation of shipment to Israel and burial there. You'll agree that a yellow forklift hoisting a box purportedly containing what's left of your own great-grandpa is truly memorable—it would definitely make a strong impression on a three-year-old, especially one obsessed at the time with vehicles of all sorts, the less frequently encountered the wheels, the more wonderful. It seems to me that I also remember thinking, as I witnessed that plain pine coffin levitating on the forklift, that it was a very small container for a grown man—maybe three feet or so in length at most, the size of a crate of rifles or Uzis, say. But who knows? My goal is to be extra scrupulous in these pages. That impression could also have been an embellishment after the fact that I later processed and incorporated as memory.

In the end, as I subsequently learned, the coffin was not shoved into the belly of the plane with the rest of the cargo—all those other coffins destined for burial somewhere in the Holy Land, suitcases destined for the land of the lost, and so on. Rather, it traveled first class, buckled into a window seat due to the unlikelihood that it would need to get up to use the facilities and bother anyone. Alongside it, in the aisle seat, sat its escort, my father, Dustin Gam, the eldest grandson. Fellow passengers who glimpsed them simply assumed that he was just another prodigy Jewish fiddler and that the case strapped in the seat next to him contained his Strad, too precious to be dumped in with the freight. The best of certified kosher cuisine was served to both of them on the finest china, since they paid full price for two tickets, and their wineglasses were never allowed to remain empty. Most of the time, though, a heavy curtain was drawn around them, not only for privacy, but in deference to those members of the priestly caste traveling on the same flight, even in steerage, who are forbidden contact or proximity with the dead.

When they landed, the limos were waiting on the tarmac. They were greeted by a full delegation of the highest level of political and religious leaders in somber black suits, many of whom had been or hoped to become beneficiaries of endowments from the Weiner Foundation, who were waiting to carry out the mitzvah of escorting the dead. The caravan headed directly to Jerusalem, to the Mount of Olives, for burial in the plot reserved for my great-grandfather, alongside the grave already occupied by his wife, Judi, who had been waiting there for him faithfully for so long.

The Mount of Olives, as everyone knows, is the number one place for a Jew to be buried, because it is here, according to the prophet Zekhariah, that the resurrection will begin. From the Mount of Olives, it would be an easy roll for the raised dead, down the slope to Jerusalem through the Golden Gate, the first to greet the messianic age. As for all the other Jews, wherever they end up, even those buried at the far-flung edges of the globe or reduced to ashes scattered in the wind, at that glorious hour they will be obliged to tunnel through the earth to the Mount of Olives and to emerge like moles blinking in the celestial light in order to partake of the redemption. Therefore, it is not only a great privilege but also a definite logistical advantage to get into the Mount of Olives—it is an incredibly elite club, but to my great-grandfather's credit I must note here that even if fate had not provided him with the means to be interred in this most exclusive of burial grounds, he still would have stipulated his desire to be laid to rest somewhere in Israel, I believe, because Israel was where he was originally from. He was born Yisrael Ganzgut in Beit HaMita, a rigidly atheistic kibbutz in the north. Dust you are and to dust you will return. This is among God's punishments of his creations for tasting the forbidden fruit of the tree of knowledge of good and evil in the book of Genesis, and my great-grandfather was a golem made of one hundred percent Israeli dust.

By the time my great-grandmother Judi met him, however, he had Hebraized his surname, as is the custom with many Israelis, in order to purge themselves of the oppressed mentality of diaspora and exile. He was now called Yisrael Gamzu. She was eighteen years old, on her post–high school year in Israel at a posh academy for young ladies endowed by her father, when she saw him for the first time. Needless to say, the administrators of the school attended to her well-being with extra diligence, they looked after her with eagle eyes. She first saw my great-grandfather during an organized tour of the ultra-pious Jerusalem neighborhoods of Mea Shearim and Geula. The girls were cautioned to dress modestly in anticipation of this visit—sleeves down to the wrists, skirts down to the ankles, stockings, and so on, in order not to arouse the urges or offend the morality of the locals, as signs everywhere warned. Great-Grandpa Izzy was begging on Malhei Israel Street in his usual spot in front of a pizza shop, near Sabbath Square. He was brought there every morning by the Breslover Hasidim who had adopted him—captured his soul and given meaning to his existence, restored his willingness to continue in this life after he had lost much of the lower half of his body when his tank was blown up in the Sinai Desert during the 1973 Yom Kippur War. It was they who convinced him that he should consider himself among the most blessed to be rid of the base animal portion of the self, the source of so much filth and temptation, and therefore it made sense to go on living. It was also they who had encouraged him to change his name to Gamzu, evoking the Talmudic figure, Nahum Ish Gamzu, whose famous motto was, *Gam zu le-tova*—in other words, "This, too, is for the best"—no matter what the misfortune.

Each morning, not counting the Sabbath of course, the Breslovers lifted him up and set him down like a tree stump in a rusted-out red Radio Flyer child's wagon that had somehow found its way to Jerusalem, the final dumping ground for all of civilization's detritus. Singing all the way the words of Rabbi Nahman of Bratslav that the whole world is a very narrow bridge and the main point and principle is not to be afraid at all, they pulled him in the wagon to his spot on Malhei Israel Street and parked him there for the day with enough food and water to suffice. When they picked him up in the evening, he never disappointed, his bucket was always filled to the brim with cash and coins. It was into this bucket that my great-grandmother Judi folded a one-hundred-dollar bill on the day she first laid eyes on him. It was the very same bill that her father had handed to her to give to charity when she arrived safely in Israel, appointing her thereby an emissary dispatched to carry out a mitzvah to whom no harm could therefore come.

"Yes, I am he and no other, Yehudit," he said, responding to the question she had asked herself but not voiced out loud as to whether he was the needy soul for whom the money she was carrying had been intended. She fingered her gold Hebrew name necklace, and raised her eyes to take him in. His face was sublimely beautiful and holy, she felt, even beyond the romance of suffering. The skin was almost golden and flaw-lessly smooth, hairless, signifying, she believed, an unmarried state. His large eyes seemed black in color, as if the pupils had overflowed, with heavy lashes, long and rich. She was mes-merized especially by the mouth, lips swollen and pursed into a heart shape reminding her of the rich pout of the Hindu gods in erotic poses carved into the facades of the temples of Khajuraho in India pictured in the glossy album that she and a girlfriend would pore over every night, illuminated by a flashlight, in a summer camp that resembled a five-star resort. Her father the Holocaust survivor had sent her there to get her out of the way while he divorced her manic-depressive mother (also a survivor whom he had met in a displaced-persons camp after the war and married there out of loneliness, to fill the void left by his first wife and three children gassed in Belzec), and the very next day, traded up by paying off a rabbi very handsomely to make it official with Yuki the geisha from Tokyo. The beggar—Yisrael Gamzu, he said his name was when she wondered silently—wore a white crocheted yarmulke pulled low over his forehead, tight-fitting like a bathing cap, from either side of which flowed his *peyot*, a dark silken lock of hair of extraordinary length, trailing down along each side of his truncated body and pooling like the train of a wedding gown or the wax of a melting candle on the floor of the wagon. His upper body, what was left of him—neck, chest, arms, a slab of hip, in its white shirt overlaid by his *tzitzit*, his long-tasseled ritual garment like a bulletproof vest—was impressively muscular and well developed, no doubt as a result of the physical effort constantly demanded of him to pump the handles of the cart or scooter or whatever contraption he generally used to get around on his own, she imagined.

She began to return every day, always accompanied by a chaperone from her program whom she paid off to slip away and pass the time window shopping up and down the streets. The head administrator, reporting on her progress to her father, noted with pleasure that Judi/Yehudit was working very diligently on original research for her final project on the ultra-religious sects of Jerusalem, under strict supervision by staff of course, and seemed to be enjoying and benefiting from the experience thoroughly.

The first thing she would do when she arrived was place a rolled-up bill in one of his two collection buckets—the one designated for money, she hoped—always American dollars, green. For the remainder of the time she would stand there conversing with him—she not uttering a single word, and he responding to her out loud, indicating that he had heard her. To a bystander it might have sounded like a telephone conversation in which you could hear only one side and must extrapolate the other. And indeed, years later, when mobile phones became ubiquitous, my great-grandmother dubbed him Mister OC, Mister Original Cellphone, or MC/BC, Mister Cellphone Before Cellphones. It was not prophetic powers that he possessed, she believed, or some kind of divine gift. Rather, it was as if he were a central control tower picking up frequencies wherever he happened to be, receiving transmissions that for him were always in range.

This power never left him. Great-Grandmother Judi, I've been told, could always tell when he got a "call." His eyes would widen in an alerted way, he would clear his throat in anticipation of talking, as if he had just heard the phone ring. He also had the power to send "calls" or messages from uncharted places, like an oracle, startling recipients in faraway lands. She could not say if he had acquired this ability as a result of the devastating injury he had endured, when he was effectively sliced almost in half like a loaf of bread and for a period of time his spirit was likely wandering in another sphere that sensitized him to vibrations not graspable by the rest of us. What she valued about it, though, what impelled her to come back to stand by his wagon day after day, what seized her and attached her to him so desperately, was her sense that here was a man who always knew what she wanted without her being forced to endure the degradation of actually having to tell him.

There was so much to talk about, really. Never before had she conversed with anyone, much less a man, with such ease, as if she had known him all her life, though she did not utter a single word aloud. They communicated in English, which he had studied in school as all Israelis were required to do, but which he perfected during his more than two years of rehabilitation following his injury by watching American films at every opportunity, especially *The Godfather*, so that he ended up sounding like an actor pretending to be a gangster, talking out of the side of his mouth. Another favorite of his was *The Exorcist*, which he also knew by heart. She looked like the possessed child from that movie, he told her, meaning it as a spiritual compliment.

Nothing was off limits between them. He answered all her unvoiced questions, considered seriously all her unspoken revelations and opinions, plucking them from the airwaves. The 1973 war destroyed his generation, he responded. Cut our stem from our root. He was the mascot. She was the fallout of the Holocaust and Hiroshima, he said after reflecting on the stories of her mother and her stepmother. Two big H's—like Ha Ha. It earned her no points, however, it was just bad luck, theirs, hers, his. The Hasidim? Innocents and clowns. But they took him in, they took care of him, he could have gone back to his kibbutz, sure, but these holy fools regarded him as a saint, there were rewards to being handled like a fat little Buddha doll, they believed him to be blessed among mortals for having been relieved of all of his gross nether parts, but what they don't realize is that the grossness resides not down there—he indicated the space of absence—but up here, and he tapped his forehead. Every morning they gave him two pails, one for what he would let out during the day and the other for what he would take in. Sometimes he mixed them up, not just for a prank but also as a teaching. The doctors who fixed him up— geniuses, like all Jewish doctors, it goes without saying, with golden hands—reconfigured his plumbing so, yes, in answer to her unspoken question, all of his pipes work fine, yes, he had been assured that he is equipped to procreate, yes, she can bring him home with her to America as hand luggage and carry him through customs valued at fifty silver shekels in the holy shekel of the sanctuary for a male over the age of twenty suitable for going to war, souvenir of Israel.

She called her father and informed him that she had met someone. She was quitting the program and bringing him home next week. They intended to be married as soon as possible. She wanted a big wedding, with all the trimmings, he should give the orders to his flunkies without delay to start the ball rolling. "Is he Jewish?" her father asked. "That's all what I wants to know." She was happy to inform him that, yes, he was, one hundred percent. "Thanks God," he exhaled, "that's all what matters, the main thing, number one," never making the connection to his own Japanese wife, who, it is true, had obeyed his orders to the letter in this as in all things before their marriage, and undergone a super-strict conversion that no one dared question.

When she arrived at the airport, he was there waiting for her with Yuki at his side holding a white orchid. "Nu, so where's your big hoo-hah already?" her father demanded. Judi pointed to Yisrael Gamzu, perched in a wheelchair beside her, pushed by an airport employee. He was like a shopping bag from duty free; whoever pays attention to such a thing? When it sank in at last, her father slammed his forehead hard with the heel of his palm. "*Oy vey iz mir!*" he cried. "What about Jewish consti-pation?" He meant Jewish continuity, my great-grandmother was always delighted to explain whenever she recounted this story, just mixing up the systems, subconscious association (this according to family legend—I, of course, never heard it myself). "You want for Hitler that *momzer* he should be the winner?" he went on. "It's the end from the Jewish people. Hitler, I'm telling you—he's laughing his head off in hell right this minute you should know, thanks to you. This is what you brings home to me? Tell me—can he do a man's business? Does he still have all his equipment? He looks to me like a fire hydrant. You know what you gets if you parks your *tukhes* by a fire hydrant? Not even a *shpritz,* not even a little *shpritz* what makes you feel nice. A big fat ticket, that's all you gets when you parks by a fire hydrant, and dog kaka, you should excuse me, all over your shoes."

Nevertheless, they were married within three months at a sumptuously lavish affair held at one of Sigi Weiner's five-star Manhattan hotels. He yielded to his high-strung daughter as he never did in business, despite his grievous reservations about this pitiful specimen of manhood she had brought home to him in a handbasket. She got his consent because, best-case scenario, he worried that she might run away to a hippie commune with this stuffed turkey in her knapsack and live in sin, if that was possible (he couldn't figure out the mechanics); at worst, she might try to throw herself out of the window of one of his skyscraper properties as her nutcase mother so often had threatened to do, leaning over the ledge.

To mark his entrance into his new life, my great-grandfather Americanized his name to Isadore Gam. Within ten years, Izzy begat five children, two sons and three daughters, all named for brothers and sisters of Sigi Weiner and his certified, by then comfortably institutionalized, mental patient ex-wife, Judi's mother, who were killed in the Shoah: Shraga, Pinya, Genya, Hatsche, and Aidel. Shraga, my grandfather, changed his name to Sean and begat two sons, my father Dustin and my uncle Dylan. Dustin begat me, Ian, his eldest, and about five years later, with his second wife, he begat my half-sister Isadora, born not quite two years after the death of our great-grandfather Izzy Gam and the torturous effort to lay him to rest that gripped the attention of the world as it played itself out.

It began on the Mount of Olives where his open grave awaited him, two mounds of earth rising on either side, a welcoming committee consisting of the head caretaker and rabbi stationed there waiting to facilitate his entry into this distinguished society of fellow dead. His body was removed from the hearse on a stretcher-like bier, no longer in its coffin but wrapped like a stuffed cabbage in his prayer shawl, and carried by experienced bearers down a meandering rocky path through the ancient tombstones, fallen and leaning and crumbling, as though through an old foul-smelling mouth with rotting teeth to be implanted in its designated cavity. Carefully and respectfully, it was lifted from the stretcher, then lowered into the open grave that awaited it by the practiced workers taking extra pains under the scrutiny of the prestigious entourage that had followed in its wake. My father, as the only living kin present for the occasion, was given a spade and honored to be the first to perform the truest act of loving kindness by covering his grandfather, settling in there at the bottom of the pit waiting to be released to go to his world and be collected back to his fathers.

Just as my father stuck the spade into one of the mounds to fill it with earth, his cell phone rang, much to his embarrassment. Damn, he must have forgotten to turn it off. He stopped for a moment to rectify this lapse, and while doing so out of habit glanced at the screen to see who was calling. It read "Grandpa." Somebody, probably his spiteful wife, my mother, must have gotten hold of Izzy's cell phone and was using it to mortify him by calling at this most awkward of times, her sick idea of a joke. She knew exactly where he was and what was going on; the whole family, the entire congregation and community for God's sake, were watching on their screens half a world away. He quickly switched off the phone—if only he could shut her off as easily, with a swift flick like this—then stabbed his shovel backward into the mound with striking force, heaped it with dirt and dumped it on the body. The phone rang again. Stepping away as others took turns with the spades to fill the grave, my father moved to the side, and concealing his mouth with the open parenthesis of one hand, answered the call.

"It's me, the human cell phone, you can't turn me off." It was the unmistakable voice and accent of my great-grandfather Izzy Gam. "Get me out of here this minute. This grave is occupied territory. There's already another dead body buried in here, right under me."

There followed a frantic consultation between my father and the graveyard officials, with the delegation of bigshots looking on miserably under the merciless sun—no toilets, no place to sit down, no snack bar, no nothing. Another *meshuggeneh* landing in the Holy Land for their sins—when would it ever end? The emergency conference resulted in the dispatching of two Arab boys into the depths of the grave. They climbed out a short while later, covered with dirt, black as coal miners, to report that there was not one body under my great-grandfather Izzy—there were three, and counting. To make matters worse, at least one of them was clearly a woman, judging from the skeleton, a completely intolerable situation, and for added proof they displayed a human foot they had brought up with them with long twisted toenails, horned claws flecked with polish that the pious ladies of the holy society preparing the dead for burial must have failed to remove; maybe it had been a busy day, maybe there had been a pogrom. Great-Grandpa Izzy was immediately extracted from that hole and set down again on the stretcher.

It would be necessary to find a new gravesite for him on the Mount, completely empty and uninhabited. Compounding the problem, it had to be exactly adjacent to another plot, also vacant, into which his wife Judi could be moved. As the search proceeded, the Arab workers fanning out across the slope of the mountain to sound its depths, the members of the VIP delegation slipping guiltily away one by one, Great-Grandpa Izzy waited inside the hearse, in a large picnic cooler packed with ice, which the driver, fortunately as it turned out, had brought along and which he was now obliged to empty of its six-packs of Maccabee beer, the he-man's brew. My father Dustin never left Great-Grandpa Izzy's side, taking upon himself the duties of watching over the dead until safely deposited out of the way, pulling up the collar of his jacket against the cold, as night set in, and against the blasts of decay coming from the stiffening body each time it was taken out of the cooler to a newly discovered, potentially suitable location. Every attempt, without fail, resulted in the phone ringing. *Ocupado.* Taken. Someone got here before me. There's already a crowd. The worms are already fat. Get me out of here right away. I don't like the company. I like my privacy. It's not dignified. I cannot rest here. This place is not my place.

My father could have ignored it, he could simply have ordered the remains, kicking and screaming, to be covered with two meters of solid earth, turned his back, and walked away, but then the human cell phone would never have stopped ringing, an intolerable tinnitus would perpetually fill his ears until his head would explode, a shrill wailing and howling would haunt him forever. He had made the initial mistake of letting people know who was calling and what the problem was, of assuring them of the reality of the situation no matter how bizarre it seemed, or alternatively, of allowing them to humor and indulge him as they would any other super-rich eccentric; in any event, there was no telling what other lines of communication Great-Grandpa Izzy was capable of accessing, he was a complete loose cannon. Now, in the name of family honor, my father had no choice but to follow through and do the right thing, there was no place to hide. By the next morning, after a relentless search through the night for an empty spot, a definitive conclusion was reached on the part of cemetery administrators in consultation with my father that there was no room left on the Mount of Olives for Great-Grandpa Izzy. The Mount of Olives was nothing but a landfill, an elevated dump made up of the decomposed waste matter of the dead barely separated by token layers of dirt, like Fresh Kills on Staten Island, a mountain of rubble smeared with the sorrow of human remains.

It was imperative to dispose of the old man as quickly as possible, not only because this is mandated by Jewish law and tradition, but most pressingly because of the rapidly deteriorating state of the corpse. What was so amazing, my father would always say later when recalling these events through the sediment of the years, in a story that had by then been sculpted with finality into an epic song of which he was the troubadour, its lyrics carved in cement, was how fast a body can begin to stink, even just half a body, even the supposedly good half. But at the time, the pressure was acute, Great-Grandpa Izzy was driving my father crazy, he was the ultimate nudnik, there was no way to shut him up. The whole planet had unfortunately already by then been alerted to this weird supernatural telepathic case of communication from the other world, the masses were beginning to tune in, to sit back to enjoy this latest episode in the long-running comic saga of the Wandering Jew as it was unfolding before their eyes. Once it became clear that the Mount of Olives was not an option, the fallback became Jerusalem. At least let's find a place for what was left of the old man somewhere in the holy ground of the earthly Jerusalem—that became the rallying cry, the consolation prize, like Pittsburgh.

The first and most obvious thought was to take him to Mount Herzl, the Mountain of Remembrance, and to unload him there—either in the military cemetery for fallen heroes or in the section allocated to Jewish leaders, notably prime ministers of Israel and Zionist laureates. Great-Grandpa Izzy was a veteran of a terrible war, and though it is true he hadn't fallen in battle, half his body had, and now he required only half a grave, it wasn't asking so much. A case could be made. And yes, strictly speaking he was not a Jewish leader, but he gave huge sums to Israel in charity, for instance, to the Breslover Hasidim who had once so selflessly taken him in and cared for him—thereby with his philanthropy relieving the State of the burden of subsidizing this constituency whom some citizens so erroneously labeled draft-dodging lunatic parasites, and at the same time, through his donations, enabling the Breslovers to continue their good works, such as—and this was just one of their projects—fulfilling the mitzvah of beautifying the land by adorning the walls separating Jewish from Palestinian areas with messianic posters heralding the imminent arrival of their holy founder, the great romantic mystic Rabbi Nahman from Uman. But these benefactions were as nothing alongside the amount of money Great-Grandpa Izzy invested in developing alternative energy sources in Israel, particularly from the gases emitted by dead bodies, which even before his passing he was already convinced to be far and away the main component of the underground holy land—wherever your foot trod, Israel's main natural resource, the dead, an energy source potentially richer than the vast oil fields of Saudi Arabia. Something could be negotiated on Mount Herzl, my father believed, it was doable, but it had to be fast, not least because the odyssey of this corpse had become a worldwide sideshow and spectacle, this was not something we Jews needed, it was making Israel look ridiculous. All it required was some money—and our family had plenty of money.

On the night of the second day, at the highest levels, in secret chambers, the order was handed down. In the pitch darkness of midnight, in a commando-like operation, a grave was dug at an undisclosed spot on top of Mount Herzl somewhere between the fallen heroes and the eminent personages of the nation. Great-Grandpa Izzy was hoisted out of the cooler by just one giant, lugged under the arm like a sack of onions, and dumped into the waiting pit. Just as my father thought he might be home free, as he always liked to tell it (but later, only later), the cell phone rang. "Are you kidding me? No way you're parking me down here. One hundred percent deads. What? You can't hear the yelling and screaming?" The minute he was returned to the surface, the phone rang again. "And Doosten'le"—Great-Grandpa Izzy always pronounced my father's name "Doosten"; *What kind of name is Doosten anyway?* he used to comment according to family lore—"when all this is over, call my CEO right away and tell him to start drilling immediately in this mountain, not to waste a minute. It's a very rich vein, full of gas—especially on the bigshot side."

For the same money, the cortège (now increased by the first wave of press armed with all manner of video and photographic gadgetry) then proceeded to the backup plan—the nearby Holocaust remembrance center, Yad Vashem, the memorial to ultimate destruction from which, like a phoenix rising from the ashes, the symbol of hope emerged as represented by Mount Herzl. Waved past one security barrier after another, they drove swiftly through the compound directly to the elevated rails on top of which was displayed a cattle car used to transport Jews to their fate, the color of rust, perched on the brink over the valley of the shadow of death. The doors of one of our caravan's cars flung open even while the vehicle was still in motion, and four men jumped out bearing spades and shovels and pickaxes. Quickly, they set to work digging a hole in the slope under the tracks concealed by the evergreens. My great-grandfather's road trip was turning into a crisis, a mega-embarrassment for the State of Israel, the old man could go on wandering and complaining like this for forty years, his cell phone did not need to be recharged, his was a battery that would never run out, it was necessary to shut this joker up once and for all. The phone rang instantly, right after Great-Grandpa Izzy was lifted out of the cooler and realized where he was. "Are you kidding me? Don't even think about it. This place is loaded, off limits—verboten."

The next stop involved a spectacularly bold move for which a substantial increase in cash upfront was required to be distributed to those parties who had declared themselves willing and able to pull it off. For this one, Great-Grandpa Izzy didn't even have to bother calling. Because as soon as they started digging a hole near the plaza of the Knesset where dead prime ministers lie in state in anticipation of being transported to their final resting place, and someone (the press had been barred) just with his cell phone snapped a picture that in no time at all lit up in the four corners of the globe, the whole mad scheme collapsed with a deafening crash.

Cries of outrage reverberated throughout the land. How could anyone even think of defiling the Knesset, the Israeli parliament of all things, the beacon of nationhood and normalcy, in such a way? Calls for an investigation into the source of this corruption were heard everywhere, from the pundits in the media to the academies and the salons, to the falafel shacks in the townships and the whorehouses at the bus stations. For the first time in the history of the State, all of its various right-to-return constituencies were united—secular and religious, Ashkenazi and Sephardi, right and left, and so on and so forth. Especially incensed were the religious parties on behalf of all the members of the priestly caste, the kohanim, among them also some Knesset comrades, who would no longer be allowed to walk these grounds or enter these halls by virtue of the precincts being contaminated by the dead. Little did they know, as Great-Grandpa Izzy remarked to my father soon after this incident, when he called just to chat, what they're sitting on top of. The hill is still heaving from all the centuries of rotting going on underneath. Great-Grandpa Izzy Gam had descended into the belly of the land, and he saw that the land was filled to overflowing with the dead it had eaten. And interestingly, it was the kohanim as a group—that is to say, those religious members of the sub-tribe of priests who still took their duties seriously—who, after these events involving my great-grandfather, were among the first to conclude that there was no choice for them but to emigrate, to regretfully descend from the Promised Land; thanks to having had their eyes opened wide by Great-Grandpa Izzy, it began to sink in that all of Israel was already a graveyard and therefore impermissible.

It's probably not necessary to add, but I feel obliged to do so here anyway for the sake of completeness, that during this leg of that fearful journey to bury my great-grandfather, attempts were also made to set him down in the more conventional cemeteries of Jerusalem and its environs, such as Sanhedria inside the city itself and Har HaMenuhot on its fringe. Each of these attempts was inevitably foiled by the ring of the telephone. The dead had moved in and taken over the city, they had besieged her and conquered her, they were her bosses, they were in control, they had triumphed. With each ring my father sank lower to the ground, his head in his hands, like a mourner in the classic panels by the rivers of Babylon, condemned to everlasting longing for thee, O Jerusalem.

The next two days—days four and five—were devoted to traveling the length and breadth of the land, raking it over in a futile search for one little spot that had not already been planted with its dead, just big enough to accommodate half a man. Israel as a country is very small; it's possible to cover the ground thoroughly in forty-eight hours divining for the dead with rods that never once move out of their painfully contorted crossed position. As a cemetery, on the other hand, Israel is very large, the largest (not only Jewish) cemetery in the world, as the UNESCO Heritage citation later confirmed. They traveled in an impressive entourage, their entire journey broadcast live by television news cameras in helicopters hovering overhead, a transfixed world nailed to their screens, tracking every minute in fascination. The rear of their caravan was made up completely of press and media, far outnumbering the main actors in this drama riding in front. One enterprising reporter even managed to get hold of Great-Grandpa Izzy's cell phone number and rang it up. Finally, someone answered. "Any comment?" she asked. "Just consider this a case of another stiff-necked Jew who won't quit until he makes his point," the voice at the other end said.

At the head of the main body of the cortège, and also behind, separating it from the press, a police car rode, with lights flashing and sirens shrieking even in the wilderness, where there was no one to give way but the jackals. More officers flanked both sides, astride their noble motorcycles, snorting and foaming. Directly behind the lead police car came Great-Grandpa Izzy in his hearse, then a long black limousine transporting my father and various important political and religious figures who slipped in and then slipped out along the way, joining to make an appearance, duly acknowledged in the nonstop coverage, followed by the van carrying the crew of workers with their dowsing and digging tools. Great-Grandpa Izzy's hearse was actually a white Tnuva dairy company refrigerated truck, donated for the occasion due to the high visibility and free advertising the event was likely to engender. The driver, however, was deeply upset at this disruption of his schedule, he took great personal pride in his punctuality and reliability, he was hoping to win a best employee award, and therefore he insisted on stopping along the way to make his deliveries of milk and cheese and butter, which in turn triggered a warning from the religious far right to the devout to refrain immediately from eating anything coming off this vehicle, where meat and milk were so flagrantly mixed and exchanging fumes in the same icy cocoon, and as an added precaution, to abstain until further notice from all products of this company, which had now come under suspicion with regard to the strictness of its adherence to kosher standards.

By the morning of the sixth day, just as my father was despairing that he'd ever unload the old man and might even need to haul him back to the States or drop him into the sea, Great-Grandpa Izzy called. "Since we're in the north already, why don't we stop off at my old kibbutz, Beit HaMita? I know there's no room at the inn for me there either, like everywhere else in the land of Israel, but you know? I'm feeling a little nostalgic. It's where my lost lower half got its best workout, before I was drafted into the army at age eighteen."

In all the years since he'd left this home of his youth, Great-Grandpa Izzy had never returned, the memories of himself young and whole were too painful to stir up, so it was a resounding shock when they arrived there to see how the place had changed. Had it not been in the same spot, and had the sign at the entrance not stated that they had reached the correct destination, it would have hardly been possible to believe that they were there at all. The idealized image of the pastoral kibbutz imprinted in memory had been utterly eradicated. In its place stood what looked like a small town, with an industrial and business center, including a shopping mall containing a respectable sampling of the familiar chain stores and a food court, as well as a five-star hotel and spa. Deeper into the interior, the communal dining room was nowhere to be seen, the barns and silos and all evidence of agricultural enterprise were also gone, the fields themselves into the distance were covered with rows of substantial private homes and villas, rich green lawns scrolling out in front, gleaming cars and vans preening at curbs and in the driveways, like any other prosperous aspiring suburb.

Farther in, though, the most remarkable sight of all was revealed—the cemetery. It had been reconfigured into family plots on streets that followed the same plan as in the kibbutz itself. On top of each plot stood a monument—an exact replica, down to the most minute detail, of the family home, a minihouse, complete with mini-landscaping and mini-vehicles, perfect copies but in miniature. The moment this marvel came into view my father's cell phone rang. "You can stop worrying, Doosten'le, I just figured it out," Great-Grandpa Izzy declared. "It's all about real estate—on the ground, under the ground, above the ground. And I know real estate. Didn't I learn at the feet of the number one landlord of all time, your great-grandfather Sigi Weiner, may he rest in peace? Take me right away back to Jerusalem, to your Grandma Judi. She's waiting. The answer is so simple—such a pity I wasted all that money on long distance."

They made it back to the Mount of Olives by mid-afternoon of the sixth day. Right on cue, my father's cell phone rang, just as they were pulling up at the side of the roadway overlooking the gravestones terracing down the slope. This would be Great-Grandpa Izzy's final communication from the other world, and, as it happened, also his longest. He was so proud of the problem he had identified and the solution he had come up with, he savored the moment and could not resist prolonging it. "So here's the deal, Doosten'le, I could kick myself for not thinking of it sooner and giving you so much aggravation with all this running around. What do you do when there's no room left on the ground, or underneath? You build up, of course, you go vertical, like New York. Here on the Mount of Olives you build up toward the heavens, toward the heavenly Jerusalem—multilevel tombs—bingo! That's the answer in a graveyard like this. So put me on top of Great-Grandma Judi, it was always our favorite position anyway, ha ha. No, all kidding aside—I mean it, just pile my tomb on top of hers, like playing with blocks, and on top of me you can pile the next tomb for the next one from our family to go, God forbid, may it not happen until one hundred and twenty years, and so on and so forth, one on top of the other, you get the picture, right? There's no limit to the possibilities, no limit to how high you can go, higher and higher, the view will be spectacular, no limit to what you can do with this concept, high-rise graveyards, family condo mausoleums, skyscrapers for the dead, the possibilities are endless. And if you're worrying about the rabbis, Doosten'le, I can tell you from where I am that I happen to know it's one hundred percent kosher by them—niches like little cubicles in an office, boxes of bones—it's an old story, check it out. So just put me in a refrigerator while you special order a nice tomb for me that, mind you, should fit elegantly and perfectly like a Lego piece on top of your grandma Judi, I don't want no toppling over. No rush, though, I can wait, I'm not going anywhere, and she doesn't have an appointment at the beauty parlor either, so far as I know. She waited for me this long, she can wait a little bit longer—right? And if any of those rabbis makes a fuss about how bad it looks to delay the burial even more, especially in such a high-profile case like this one, tell them that if it was good enough for Father Jacob, it's good enough for me. If he could wait, I can wait also. Just tell them from me to check out the book of Genesis, chapter fifty, verses two and three."

With these words of Torah Great-Grandpa Izzy rested. The cited passage contained the description of the embalming of the dead patriarch in Egypt by order of his son, the grand vizier Joseph, to preserve what was left of the old man until he could be transported back to Canaan to be buried as promised alongside his fathers in Hebron. My father had dutifully looked it up.

Ah, a can of worms—that's what Great-Grandpa Izzy had opened and released in every sense. Within the year, the land-scape of the Holy Land began to change strikingly. Soaring high-rises for the dead shot up everywhere. A new market was opened as aggressive real estate speculators, many of them Jewish, seized the idea that emerged from the painful truth exposed by the public failure to find a resting place in Israel for my great-grandfather, and ran with it. At the same time, as more and more people left the land, contractors, architects, interior designers, and other such innovative and creative specialists moved in to remodel the abandoned living quarters and transform them into suitable private or family burial spaces to house their owners when they returned like dreamers to Zion in pine boxes.

In the immediate sense, the UNESCO Heritage declaration so widely celebrated for solving the Israel problem and at the same time saving Israel for the Jews by designating and protecting it as the world's largest Jewish cemetery might have been regarded as a brilliant conceptual leap, a stunningly original and clarifying connection. In the final sense, however, it merely confirmed what were already the facts on the ground. Because by the time the World Heritage designation was enacted and put into force, a decade or so after Great-Grandpa Izzy's extraordinarily illuminating odyssey, the land of Israel was already almost fully saturated with the dead, not only below ground, as my great-grandfather had so effectively demonstrated, but the earth itself was also groaning from the weight of all those structures rising on its surface, packed with corpses pressing down upon it. Many of these towers were by then already beginning to decay, crumbling into slums of the dead, teeming, run-down, sub-standard, heavy with pollution and toxic gases, rats and juke bugs staking their claim to the spoils of death— Israel, the country of the dead, undulating with death's court and legions, like the city of the dead in nearby Egypt where Joseph the vizier had once ruled.

The fact is, by the time the World Heritage solution was enacted, it was already becoming urgently clear that there was a limit even to how high you could go. The entire venture was threatening to come crashing down like the Tower of Babel. In anticipation of the need for new burial frontiers, pioneer businessmen, dominated by former Israelis, were already buying up great tracts of land on Mars, naming them New Israel, Holy Land Annex, Promised Land Too (II), New Zion, New Judea, and the like, already shooting off prepaid round-trip customers in their shrouds in specially designed spaceships with a guaranteed open-ended return ticket to be used hassle-free at the coming of the messiah, dropping them off to wait out the interim in longing on the cold planet in a dead zone from which we, the living, would never again be troubled by their call.

ALSO BY TOVA REICH

Mother India

One Hundred Philistine Foreskins

My Holocaust

The Jewish War

Master of the Return

Mara

ABOUT THE AUTHOR

Tova Reich is the author of the novels *Mara, Master of the Return, The Jewish War, My Holocaust,* and *One Hundred Philistine Foreskins.* Her most recent novel, *Mother India* (2018), was longlisted for the South Asia Literature Prize and was a finalist for the National Jewish Book Award. Her stories have appeared in the *Atlantic, Harper's, Ploughshares,* and elsewhere. She is the recipient of the National Magazine Award for Fiction, the Edward Wallant Book Award, and other prizes. She lives on the fringe of Washington, DC.

ABOUT SEVEN STORIES PRESS

Seven Stories Press is an independent book publisher based in New York City. We publish works of the imagination by such writers as Nelson Algren, Russell Banks, Octavia E. Butler, Ani DiFranco, Assia Djebar, Ariel Dorfman, Coco Fusco, Barry Gifford, Martha Long, Luis Negrón, Hwang Sok-yong, Lee Stringer, and Kurt Vonnegut, to name a few, together with political titles by voices of conscience, including Subhankar Banerjee, the Boston Women's Health Collective, Noam Chomsky, Angela Y. Davis, Human Rights Watch, Derrick Jensen, Ralph Nader, Loretta Napoleoni, Gary Null, Greg Palast, Project Censored, Barbara Seaman, Alice Walker, Gary Webb, and Howard Zinn, among many others. Seven Stories Press believes publishers have a special responsibility to defend free speech and human rights, and to celebrate the gifts of the human imagination, wherever we can. In 2012 we launched Triangle Square books for young readers with strong social justice and narrative components, telling personal stories of courage and commitment. For additional information, visit www.sevenstories.com.